The Termite Squad:

My Official and Authentic Report

The Termite Squad:

My Official and Authentic Report

Joan Galt

EggyPress.ca

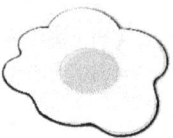

For Charmaine Clamor -- and every other beautiful soul like her trying to leave the world a better place than they found it. You are my inspiration.

Posted: 01:11:00

Status: PUBLIC

AutoFeeds: ON

It's Me

"Who is Joan Galt?"

If you're reading this, I'm assuming "who's joan galt" has been the #1 search term in the past 24 hours. Maybe for a whole week. Lots of interest. Lots of theories. *Who is Joan Galt*? I'm assuming everyone is going to want to know.

My light is ebbing, you could say. [By now it's probably snuffed out. But you never know...] Before it's extinguished completely, while I'm still able to influence what's said about me in the Twittosphere and the annals of history – which is sort of the same thing, right? -- I need to answer the "who is she?" question. Definitively.

Because I'm the only one who can.

Yes, people, this is me. **The real Joan Galt**. Not an avatar. I exist. I'm not a character the government concocted to scare you, like Pervez "Gas Man" Shah or Mindy the White Scorpion.

I'm real.

Who is Joan Galt? They'll say I was a "terrorist."

A criminal.

They'll say I was a menace to society, the toxic tumor of a diseased civilization. The news commentators and Twitlords® will offer smart-seeming theories. They'll say I was a symbol of the national mood, a receptacle for our worst fears and impulses -- or whatever sounds good at the time. They'll hashtag me #evil.

The truth is not what they're going to try to tell you when I'm dead. The truth is not the multimedia events they'll concoct or the Wiki entry repeatedly edited to their satisfaction.

The truth is I'm just a girl who wanted the world to be a better place.

My Great Idea

Before I came along, the ongoing success of the Termite Squad was built on one key assumption: Old ladies can get away with more than the average person.

Ladies in general, of course. But, especially, *old* ladies. One-hundred years or more. Centenarians. *Centurions*, as the kids say.

Have you ever met a woman born in 2000, or earlier? They like to complain. Even though life expectancy is around, like, what, 104 these days? Her lost looks, her reduced pension, her ruinous healthcare costs. And she'll remind you repeatedly about how she didn't have to desalinate everything back in the day, how water used to be free and you didn't need a wind-gathering license.

Not hating on them. Old ladies are permitted to deliver soliloquies, because they're totally entitled to. Just like they're entitled to cut in line.

They do what they want. Very few of us complain. Of course we don't! They're *old*. They're adorable. The rudeness is sort of cute in a way, like a puppy. We understand.

No one likes to say "no" to the elderly, to a frail and wizened woman who looks like your mother. No one wants to disappoint her mother.

When an old lady asks for help, she usually gets help. When an old lady asks for a little favor, some special treatment, she usually gets special treatment. Even when she's wearing an Endvest™.

My great idea was a simple idea: Keep the ladies, add the sexy.

Those were my exact words. That's exactly what I said to the Director of Operations, when they brought me in to make my pitch. I had cashed in all my banked favors and got the meeting, the face2face kind, right there in Langley. I knew I had only a few minutes to get their attention and hold it.

"Keep the ladies, add the sexy," I said, smiling my best "*I'm just a sassy little girl with a lot of moxie*" smile. It worked.

There were perfectly good reasons at first to restrict the Termite Squad to Centurions, to women

100 or more years-old. The most obvious being that they really could die any day.

Plus, everyone involved in national security knew that the Elders strategy would be detected and defeated eventually. Argentina had already started denying entry visas to foreign senior citizens with mobility issues, and chatter in the diplomatic community suggested that Malaysia and Turkey were considering similar "anti-cripple" legislation. So now Termite Squad recruiters were looking for high-mobility Centurions – ladies who didn't need a chair. But, still, the bad guys were starting to put their guard up. They were on the lookout for shriveled Super Seniors.

It occurred to me the day I got my diagnosis: Why do you have to be old to be a hero? Why can't you be a hero when you're young and vivacious and you still have your figure?

Keep the ladies, add the sexy. I'm *28*, OK? I don't look like the usual Termite.

I have above-average Liker stats. Above-average WorthScore©. Not bragging, but thanks to a fairly extensive network of personal feeds, my profile has been shared on the Home Page of some very important sites. #justbeingreal

I dated Ladante Mook (briefly) and Garreth Sparks (slightly longer), and that's not to mention some of my fleeting hook-ups, which I'm sure you're already checking. Search away. I'm not one to kiss and post. But at this point…I guess I can reveal that I had one (dreamy) night with Harry Spenser – and no, I'm not kidding. Check your arm. Put in our two names + Mumbai. You'll see. And yes, it was everything you would imagine it would be. Like one of his movies, but real. #delicious.

Eventually, I connected with the man of my dreams, my JJ, and those boys became nothing to me but fond memories. But I wouldn't trade them.

The point is looks matter. Right? Youth matters. I didn't make the rules. I just play by them.

So I impressed upon the Director that a potential Termite's ability to *gain access* was what made her valuable. The more access to powerful people the better. I told him, "Not many people can say 'no' to a sweet old lady. Even fewer can say 'no' to a sweet young one."

The Termite Squad's Director of Operations, who was officially separated from his wife when I met him, totally got my message. Or got me. Or both. But he got it.

I hope you do, too. I hope you understand.

We're all going to die. Some of us are just meant to be an attractive corpse.

I'm kidding but I'm not. You know what I mean?

I didn't plan my life out wanting to die young. I didn't want to be a martyr. No matter how expertly you've calibrated your algo-chip, sometimes life decides certain things for you. It's out of your hands. When that happens, you just have to make the best of it.

For me, it was an easy decision. When I got the diagnosis, it was a very easy decision. I wanted to be a member of the Termite Squad.

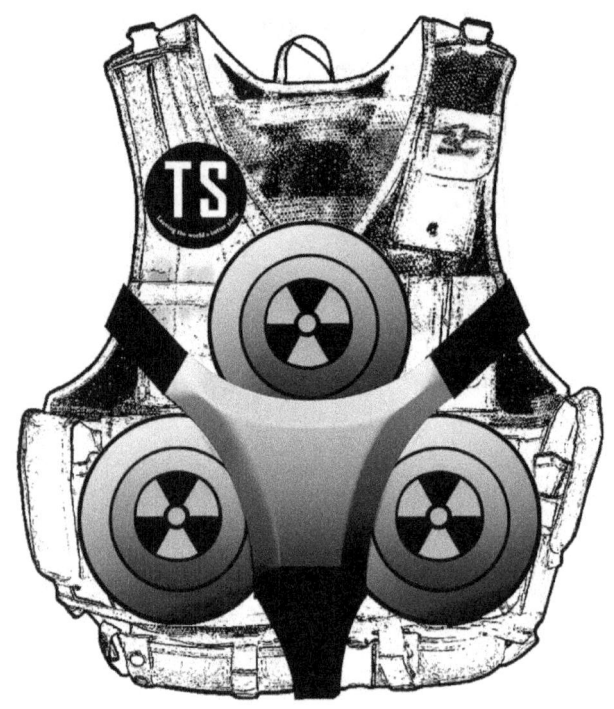

Where I Came From

Don't accept whatever "standard bio" they're going to foist on you, with all the embarrassing parts taken out. *This* is my real story. My true bio.

[Please someone take the time to run an independent review of this post's digital footprint and post the results! Now! Before they figure out how to de-authenticate me.]

Although my birth parents were never joined in holy matrimony, I consider myself quite legitimate. *Bastard* – it's such an ugly word, one of those terms that says more about the person using it than the person it's supposed to describe.

I was conceived with love, in love, as an expression of love. To some people that's not enough. To me, that's all that matters.

My birth mother Elaine adored my birth father Theo. My father adored my mother. Had they not been married to other people when they made me, their romance (and the child it produced) could have been one of those amusing old-fashioned screwball comedies of the 20th Century, a heartwarming story of opposites attracting, of ardor and passion overcoming the stifling conventions of polite society.

Somehow shame got involved and the whole cuteness factor evaporated.

My birth mother Elaine came from high society; my birth father Theo didn't. She was petite, fair, and stylish (think Trudy Wexler, especially in her Web Events of the 70s and early-80s); he was tall, dark, and famously unconcerned with fashion (think Dirk Fredericks, an incorrigible bad boy with a tremble-producing smile). Despite their dramatic difference in cumulative WorthScore©, they had an attraction to each other, a chemistry that was so obvious, so palpable, that it set off Connection Alerts® on the arms of innocent bystanders! We're talking major radiation.

I come from passionate people.

On my mom's side I've done the research, and I can trace various ancestral veins back nearly 300 years, to around 1800. Like, original white American settler people who systematically replaced the people who were there before them. The genocidal type.

They're not very interesting, my ancestors, in terms of buzz factor or heat. They were just Regulars, average non-celebs who probably wouldn't even be five-figures popular. (A few hundred Likers maybe, if that? Normal.) If you really want to know about my forebears, you can always check your Armscreen®, of course. Archival photos and everything. Even some low-definition video. Please do. You'll see that I'm not making this up.

ALERT: I'm not making *anything* up. I'd like to emphasize that again. I'm real. This is real. You'll choose to believe me or not, but I seriously hope you do. #notspoofing

These days they seem to be able to re-edit history with impressive results, but they can only go back so far before tech incompatibility makes it impossible. No matter how many Super Wipers™ you unleash on the Web, you can't modify something called the "Oral Tradition."[1] I just hope you'll believe me and not them. They're all-

---

[1] An ancient practice which involved people sharing information by talking to each other, like face2face.

powerful and they've got their ways, their persuasion techniques, but I've got TRUTH on my side, and that's supposed to count for something.

More truth: my grandparents – now, they were sort of interesting! Sure, they were born last century and had some of that charming antique adorableness about them (the "hand-held" devices, the manual inputting of TexThoughts®). But they were also somehow modern and cool.

My grandparents on my mother's side supposedly met on Election Night, 2012 – the second term for a man named Barack Obama, whose Wiki indicates he wasn't a particularly good President (one in a long line of corporate stooges) but who has a place in history as the first non-White to hold the office.[2] His daughter Malia -- Malia Obama Bieber, the inventor of Safe Kill™ -- is probably the best known of that family.

---

[2] Quick history reminder: At one point a long, long time ago, Americans weren't required to warehouse their slaves offshore. These onshore slaves produced millions of offspring, and eventually one of them became President. At the time, this was a cause for national celebration, for reasons that aren't entirely clear. They seemed to judge people by irrelevant things like their skin color, not essential content like their WorthScore©.

According to my mother, Elaine, *her* mother, my Grammy Belle, was a national student volunteer coordinator on the Presidential campaign – for the other guy! A rich handsome fellow with impeccably combed hair. Grammy Belle's father (my great-grandfather) worked for the rich guy's consulting company, specializing in firing redundant employees.

I never met Grammy Belle, or any of my grandparents. My family on that side, from what I can gather, has always been aligned with the spirit of free enterprise and entrepreneurial success. They were winners. Achievers. *Doers.* Always where the action was, where the power concentrated. I definitely inherited this trait... even though my story has turned out different.

According to my mother Elaine, Grammy Belle, who had postponed her last year at The Harvard™ to fight for American values, was so terribly upset and shocked that her righteous Republican[3] candidate lost to some "colored Socialist" (her words!) that she had a kind of nervous breakdown, complete with uncontrollable tears and weird hand spasms, right there in a fancy hotel ballroom, at what was supposed to be the victory party. A rich handsome fellow named Larry Barclay, also a student, also a national coordinator,

---

[3] Remember, this was 2012, back when they still had two parties, way before they all merged.

who would go on to be a fabulously successful banker (the family business) – well, he comforted Belle so nicely and with such obvious interest in her well-being that she eventually married him.

Corny, icky, and totally for-realzies. They gave me the romantic gene.

Within a decade Larry and Belle Barclay had three children, twin boys Jason and George, both of whom went on to legendary careers at the New York office of China Bank™, and four years later, in 2025, a baby girl, Elaine. My mother.

Let me tell you about Elaine. She was a kind of genius, with a gift for math and foreign languages and music, and by the time she had graduated from The Harvard™ she had already amassed a fortune, thanks to proprietary currency-trading software she'd created, which recognized arbitrage opportunities in the Asian and European markets – and executed the trades while she slept (or partied). She was rich and beautiful and, you can imagine, rather intimidating to the average man.

Senator Daniel Huxley was not the average man.

He was also rich (textiles) and beautiful (his mother has been a well-known actress in the days of free TV), and famously suave around the ladies. That he was nearly 25 years older than Elaine when he began courting her didn't seem to bother anyone.

Senator Huxley whisked her away on his private jet to Paris to shop for silk scarves, and to London for a proper afternoon tea, and to the Huxley family retreat in Idaho to ride expensive horses and "herd" the family's collection of rare bison. Elaine was swept off her feet, as every girl ought to be at least once in her life, and she decided that being a Senator's wife – and, it was understood, a potential First Lady of the United States of America – was a role she could get used to. "He was a dazzling man," I remember Elaine telling me, with genuine admiration. "He made me feel like a princess."

Unfortunately, Senator Huxley was also one of those rich and powerful men who occasionally enjoyed feeling like a princess himself. With young men of dubious morals.

Elaine and the Senator seemed to have had an arrangement. He could keep his playthings, who tended to be muscular and tan, and she could indulge her youthful distractions, who tended to be artsy and poor. She liked tall gaunt boys who could talk smart and last long into the night. Boys like my father.

From what Elaine has told me, little or nothing about the Barclays' private lives got discussed; the Senator and his young wife prided themselves on discretion, as though their ability to pretend that nothing was wrong with their marriage guaranteed that there would never be anything wrong with their marriage.

I don't know how many affairs my mother had, and I don't want to know. That's her business. I just know that one night in New York City she met a married painter-sculptor-collagist named Theo Galt at a gallery opening, and after a few glasses of Chardonnay and an impromptu Midnight dinner in North Chinatown, near Citi™ Washington Square Park she had what she described as "the greatest night" of her life.

The night I was created.

"He made me feel like a woman, Joanie," Elaine told me, many years later, at one of our lunches. When I had finally mustered the courage to track her down, introduce myself, and make her tell me *everything*, Elaine eventually suggested we meet for lunch, face2face in her neighborhood, in Georgetown. An actual Outdoors In-Person encounter. #OIP!

That quickly became our tradition. We had lunch with a pot of green tea at a Japanese restaurant, and she talked about the past.

Elaine enjoyed reminiscing about Theo. I liked learning about my birth father. "I can't say he was a particularly *good* man. I mean, the drinking, the promiscuity, the infidelity," she said, scrunching her nose. "But he was a *great* man. He made me feel invincibly strong and helplessly weak at the same time. Plus, I think I was in love with him – or with his art, at least."

What Theo Galt made were these smallish transparent glass boxes, like the size of an old-fashioned printed book, the kind with hard covers. Inside were strange collage-sculpture-assemblages, which he called *accumulations*. They often included highly personal effects, like faded photographs (the antique kind, on paper) or bits of his own black hair. They give off a remarkable vibrational energy, a presence.

I know this because at our very first lunch, the first time I ever looked my real mother in the eye and saw myself reflected back, Elaine gave me one of Theo's boxes. "Joan, I'm certain your father would have wanted you to have this," she had said.

Throughout her adult life she'd quietly collected most of Theo Galt's major *accumulations* that weren't already in small European museums.[4]

"I think it's one of his best," she said. When I looked inside at the peculiar world my father had created, with random items (antique pen, dried butterfly, broken water glass) that seemed to tell a story somehow, I felt as though I knew him.

---

[4] The Lynghoss outside Copenhagen has the most: Three. There's not that many out there. He died young. Runs in the family, I guess.

"That's his hair," Elaine whispered, her voice breaking. Just a few strands, a dull black, bordering bits of an illegible poem.

eerless mem   s a

happie   ws.

I could tell by the way Elaine sighed nearly 30 years after the fact that my birth father was still in her heart. He seemed like a cool guy – other than the cheating on his wife and not using birth-control part.

I never met him. When I was an infant, Theo Galt died near his Brooklyn apartment in a vehicle explosion. The car he was in blew up spontaneously, or may have struck an incendiary device. He was thought to have been killed instantly.

The few pictures I've seen – and you can see for yourself, if you want to check your arm – the pictures indicate that he was quite beautiful, with blue-green eyes and a crooked smile. People say I inherited his lips, his kissable puffy pillow lips. And his artistic temperament, supposedly. That's what people always say.

I also got his last name…Not right away, though. It's a strange story.

After falling for Elaine, Theo wanted to divorce his wife, about whom I know nothing other

18

than she supposedly was "mentally unstable," which is what people say about anyone they don't really understand or trust. They didn't have any kids (supposedly) and almost no community property. Theo the Artist wanted Elaine to divorce the Senator, move out of the mansion on the Potomac, and live the Bohemian life with him in an unsanitary place near the Brooklyn Bridge, with a mattress on the floor and candles in empty Hungarian wine bottles everywhere.

For about six months, that was the working plan. Elaine was ready for a radical change. She was going to do it!

After announcing to Senator Huxley that she had met the man of her dreams, etc., and that it would be best for all involved if things were handled discreetly, she began to formulate an outline of her new life. Her better life. My mother was quite the romantic.

Money wasn't an issue; she had plenty, and, besides, she was the kind of brainiac who could always figure out some new way to get rich. Elaine imagined that in her free time she would form nonprofit organizations to advocate for abused women; and she would learn how to play the violin; and she would raise her naturally creative daughter with the same love and kindness and maternal devotion she showed to her "legitimate" son Daniel, Jr., about to turn five.

"I convinced myself that I was going to keep the baby, walk away from all the Washington nonsense, and feel glad to be alive for all the right reasons," she told me. "I really was going to. That was my intention."

That would have been nice.

But eventually Elaine changed her mind. Or came to her senses, depending on how you look at it. She left Theo the Artist and returned to the Senator, all the while sporting an advanced case of pregnancy. Seeing as she was so far along, she (they?) decided to keep "it." It being me.

Every human life is a blessing, they say.

Some more than others, apparently. Allegedly over the furious objections of Theo, my birth mother Elaine Barclay Huxley and my step-father Senator Daniel Huxley, put me up for adoption.

Immediately.

They never took me home. They never named me.

Until I tracked Elaine Huxley down seven years ago, when I turned 21, I didn't know that part. Probably for the best.

No one is sure who first called me "Joan." I've heard stories about being named after Joan of

Arc, and stories about some 20th Century female rock singer, or a kind Filipina nurse who looked after me in my infancy. Maybe they're *all* true.

I spent the first three years of my life in three different foster family environments around the D.C.-area, none of which I remember. All part of the public record.

In 2065, when I was three-going-on-four, I was legally adopted by Michael Demmler (Justice Department) and Peter Rollins (National Offense Department), my two dads. I officially became Joan Demmler-Rollins.

If they knew any juicy details about my past, they never told me. My dads were (and are) total sweethearts, and they're both proudly queer – meaning, they both enjoy playing dolls and dress-up way more than their little girl. Also, in our home it was opera and Broadway show-tunes 24/7. I'm not kidding. That musical *Infinite Jest*, with all the drugs and tennis? I had it memorized by, like, six years-old.

They were lovely with me. Loving. Perfect. Two amazingly great dads.

But neither of them was my father.

I was an introverted kid, which I guess was easy to misinterpret as embittered and sad, but, really, I was just sort of shy and meditative, and I didn't ask a lot of questions. I figured out most things on my own. Like most of my adoption story. No one had to tell me.

When I was 17 going on 18, Daddy Michael and Daddy Peter had "the big talk" with me, sharing everything they knew about my past, which, trust me, wasn't much. It was weird, because nobody had ever pretended I *wasn't* adopted, but then again we never really dwelled on it or discussed it with anyone outside our immediate family. A big deal was never made.

My Dads told me what they knew – which was mostly searchable, anyway – and then they got all silent and uncomfortable and Daddy Michael said, "So, on the subject of birth origins…Joan, we think now might be a good time to have a little chat about sexual intercourse. How to be responsible during…you know."

"Dad. I'm 17! What century are you living in?"

"You know, Joanie, we always felt, your dad and I, that we should have lived in the Victorian Period," Daddy Michael said.

"With petticoats," said Daddy Peter. "When no one ever really talks about anything, but it's all *so* wonderfully suggestive, just under the surface."

I must have rolled my eyes. "Up-to-the-second *up*date," I chirped, sounding just like the one you get on your arm. "Newsflash!" I assured them

22

that whenever I had sex – and I'd been doing it since I was 15, 13 if you count girls – I was a lot more responsible than my birth mother had been.

I think that embarrassed them a little, although I could tell by the mischievous look in his eye that Daddy Michael had the urge to cackle theatrically and use the word *slut* ironically. He's fun. They both are.

I didn't mind being Joan Demmler-Rollins in any way. I was cool with it. But once I turned 21 and tracked down Elaine and found out where I *really* came from, I felt that taking my birth father's name – just as any "regular" daughter would – was the best way to honor his role in making me before he perished.

I believe what I've been told about him. I feel my birth father wanted to keep me.

I feel he would have been a great dad. I feel like he never truly wanted to give me up. He wanted me.

Daddy Michael and Daddy Peter understood. They knew I'd always be their little girl. But they also knew I was a woman now. I was my father's daughter. I was Joan Galt. And that's who I'll be until the final moment

24

There's Always a Boy

I understand. You want to know if someone put me up to this. If I'm a victim.

Answer: The only thing I'm a victim of is loving too much. Loving too deeply.

That's the truth. But I know it's not going to satisfy most of you. You want the whole story. The *dirt*.

OK. Fine. Let me ask you, though: can love, *real* love, ever be dirty? If you think it can, we're going to have a hard time connecting with each other. Because I still believe that pure love is too strong to be contaminated.

I told you I was a romantic. The hopeless kind.

Let me ask you another question. Have you ever been in love? Not "really liked a lot." Not "totally in lust with." *Loved*. Like, the one true love of your life? The person who completes you?

Then you know how I felt when I met the love of my life. I knew.

When that happened the question was not "would I do anything for him?" The question was what *wouldn't* I do for him.

But for the record, as clearly as I can state this for all posterity: **Jonah Jones did not and does not and never will support my decision.** He's probably against it.

The decision is mine. And I'm so sorry if he doesn't agree with it.

But I still love him. I always will. [I LOVE YOU, Jonah!]

And I hope he'll still love me forever, even when I'm not there.

Something You Should Know About Me

I'm pretty bad with choices. Especially now that I'm a Termite, when there's no do-overs. Too many factors to weigh, too many factors to consider and evaluate. Eligible candidates. So much. Too much.

I don't pine for the old days. I'm one of those strange people who actually like the way we do it *now,* with one of everything instead of two.

Lots of my friends prefer the old days, when you always had two choices. Like, for your shopping, Amazon™ or eStore™. Now that it's just eStore™ they're all bitter.

Doesn't really bother me that much. They both carried the same slave-made merchandise as the other one, at the same price. The only time I catch myself wishing for the ancient days of PC/Mac™, is when I'm forced to do outdoors shopping, which is at least once or twice a year.

I can't stand going to the W-Mart™ since they did that whole "rebranding" thing. After they swallowed up Home Station™, which had previously swallowed up two or three other biggies, the atmosphere there has changed. I still don't understand why the one place to buy things (outdoors) is required by law to hire war veterans.

Every single employee? Is that necessary? #Idontgetit.

For the most part, though, I'm cool with the Single Big Box model. As a shopper. As a consumer. I get it. We all like it because it's cheaper and more convenient for us. It's just *better*.

But there's another side of the story.

One night, at one of those quaint "candlelight" dinners we liked to simulate, Jonah put his glass against his cheek and licked his lips – which usually meant he was about to say something important. I'm sure I smiled at him. I know I probably stared, seeing if I could melt him with my gaze.[5]

"Jo-Jo," he said, smiling that cute little boy smirk, the one that made it very hard to take him

---

[5] I know you've already seen the photos, obviously, but can I just say? Jonah is a beautiful man. I hope that doesn't sound too narcissistic. I'm aware that we have some similar features.

seriously, or to pay attention. "Our convenience comes at a great price. We just don't realize it, because we're not the ones who have to pay it."

"Jonah," I said, flashing my altogether-innocent-yet-so-*not* smile, the one that made it very hard for Jonah to take anything too seriously. "Considering that goods and services are being sold at an all-time low while certain commodities are at an all-time high, you could say we're living in a golden age. An age of gold."

He chuckled. I could tell he wanted to lean across the table and kiss me. "That's because the cost of slavery, labor, whatever you want to call it, is at an all-time low. Well, the lowest since the Twelve Hundreds, according to Tru-Wage©. The app."

"My darling," I murmured, staring in his blue-green eyes, which, for some reason, always made *my* eyes misty. "Nothing can be cheaper than *free*. And I'm pretty sure that the slaves we kept in the 1700s –"

" – were actually slightly more expensive, more costly, than the current version!" he interjected, smiling broadly and nodding. "Back then they had to house and feed the slaves, like livestock. Now, with, like, your average Portuguese slave, you only have to pay him, what? Like 20 rupees or 10 yuan-dollars a day – and *he's* responsible for feeding and clothing and medicating himself. When you add everything up, it's actually cheaper today than before Civil War One."

I'm not going to lie. We didn't finish the conversation at that candlelight dinner. My Connection Alerts® screen was peeping like a crate of baby grasshoppers. (I had forgotten to mute it, like some innocent virgin.) There was no way graceful way to pretend that I didn't want Jonah right then, right there, however he wanted to have me.

So we finished that discussion another day.

Before that night I knew, of course, that life isn't really fair for some people. Believe me, I understood.

But that night with Jonah was the first time I became aware that life isn't really fair for some people -- and that it's all *totally on purpose*.

Have You Been Tested?

Before you judge me, please get tested.

The results will almost surely be negative. The important thing is that you'll know. You won't have to live with a lingering annoying irritating doubt. You'll be clear on who you are, and what you are. And where you're heading.

If your diagnosis comes back like mine – well, I hope you'll do the right thing.

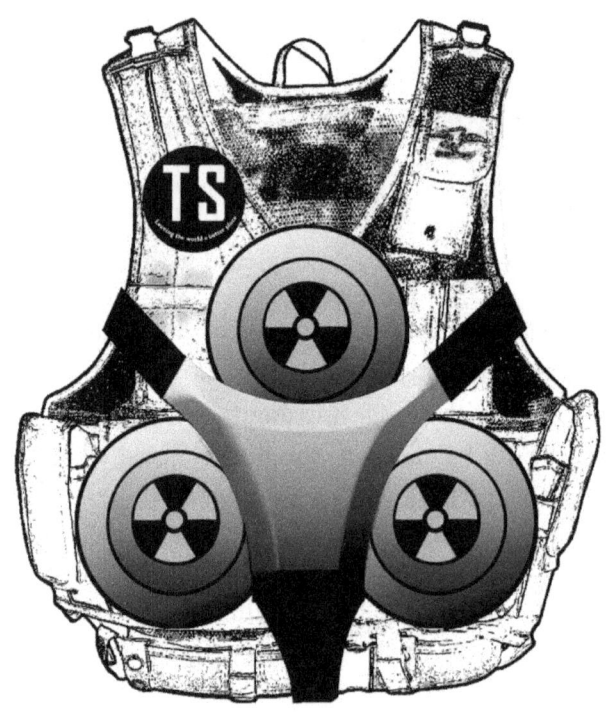

Words That Have Stayed With Me

This was early in our relationship. I didn't really know Jonah yet. I knew the broad outlines, I knew the story that searching told me on my arm, but I didn't yet know the details, the quirks. The stuff that you wouldn't find on someone's Wiki, yet it's so totally a part of who they are.

We were doing our first Outdoors In-Person date. A walk through Google™ Park (the original one, in New York). This was before I took the Agency job, before we moved to D.C. There's always that slight weirdness when you transition from network contact to OIP, but when it happened we were just naturally comfortable with each other. I felt relieved and pleasantly surprised. I thought, "I'm super attracted to this guy *and* I feel relaxed around him. This could be something."

Sometimes a girl just knows.

Our stroll was lovely. Unrushed. I noticed
that Jonah had the ability to lope along and look at
me simultaneously. He'd steal little glances at the
path, and at the statues and birds and whatever, but
his attention was on my face. Not on his arm. No
crookneck, like most guys. And also unlike most
guys, he didn't seem to be obsessed with the form-
fitting Stretchies™ I was wearing on my bottom
half. I mean, he noticed – dude, you better! -- but
didn't gawk. I found him very old-fashioned and
endearing. Very sweet.

As we walked and talked, without breaking
stride Jonah picked up every little piece of litter
within range. Empty Cloropellet™ wrappers,
tissues, joint butts – all of it plucked like ripe
strawberries and deposited into a trash barrel. Or
when there wasn't one around, his pocket.

He said nothing about his strange habit, his
compulsion to bring order to a chaotic universe. It
just seemed very normal to Jonah to be walking,
talking, and picking up litter while on a first
outdoors date.

I couldn't stop myself. "Why are you doing
that?" I asked, sweetly as I could.

Jonah smiled. "Being of service?"

"Are you going to clean up the entire park?"

He laughed. "I guess that depends on how
long of a walk you'd   like to have."

34

I felt like I wanted this walk to go on forever. But of course I didn't say that, not on a firsty. "A month," I said. "Until you get every last water box. *And* the biodegradable straw that goes with it."

"That's a lot of public service," he said. "But I like it. I feel good about doing something for others. For the park."

"So, seriously, Jonah, this is like a therapy for you?" I wondered.

Then he stopped walking. He took my hands in his and looked in my eyes. "Joan, in this life we all do whatever we can. Most of us decide that what we can do is absolutely nothing. But some of us feel we can do more than nothing. So we do something."

Then he kissed me.

Why does the world never change? Why do we keep repeating the same mistakes over and over? Why do we cause suffering? Why do we allow suffering?

Because most of us have decided that what we can do is nothing.

When enough people believe it, nothing is exactly what happens.

But when one girl *doesn't* believe it, amazing things are possible.

The Galt Thing

I am Joan Galt. Which is interesting, because I could have easily been named something else.

My great-grandparents, Theo Galt's grandparents on his dad's side, Gail and Steven Galt, according to my arm, were wacky 20th Century types who devoted themselves to tendentious allegory books that supposedly contained answers to moral questions not adequately addressed in religious tomes. *Long* books. Like, 500-pagers.[6]

In a way they *were* religious tomes. These guides were written by a mendacious adulterer who passed herself off as a high-priestess of "personal responsibility." Hilarious, I know.

---

[6] Historical reminder: Prior to 2028, publishing portals printed "books" of *any* length. The 200-pages-or-less rule was not yet in effect.

Theo's grandparents Gail and Steven were members of a ridiculous cult, now defunct, called *Objectivists*, who believed that capitalism could save the world, not destroy it. Gail and Steven were *way* into this stuff. They went to court to have their last names *changed* to Galt. Previously it was something else, although someone somewhere along the way managed to get that information permanently expunged and deleted and whatever else they can do. Result: there's no record of what their original name might have been. But they ended up Galts.

Weird, right? These were very fringe characters, and not nearly as dangerous as they sound. But definitely deranged, and I'm now sure I got some of *that* passed down to me, too.

Look it up: Their son Todd's birth certificate says "Todd Galt." And Todd's son Theo was born Theo Galt.

And I'm his daughter. Joan Galt.

And I hope that if he were around to see everything that's happened, Theo would be proud of my decision.

God's Law

You remember what a bad year 2084 was, right? One disaster worse than the previous one. Not fun. I recall thinking, "*Another* hurricane? Is this a bad dream, or is this really happening?"

Oh, it most certainly was happening. The disasters. The unrest. The arrests.

One never forgets her first time being placed in handcuffs (involuntarily). In 2084, when I was 22, I got arrested, along with, like 50,000 other people in my network. Every one of us brought up on Mass Disturbance charges.

You couldn't really blame the authorities, the people my friend Megan the Vegan likes to call the PoWeRS[7]. I've known Megan a long time, back before she refused to wax herself, back when she still ate birds and insects. I knew her back when she

---

[7] People Who Run Stuff.

was *developing shopping centers in India.* Before she got all militant. Megan understands PoWeRS, because she sort of used to be one.

Megan also used to be a party girl. We called her Miss Booty-Booty. (Don't ask!) She was fun. Whenever we would hang out in our electro-circle, with our besties Elena and Bebé, Megan could make all of us laugh at nothing. She was very light.

Then, I don't know when, she started getting heavy. Me and Bebe, we would be gossiping about nothing, sharing our private feeds, girl stuff, and Megan would get all silent and distant. She gradually steered the conversation away from boys and Mescastrips™ to whatever social justice concept was currently seducing her. The water thing. Solar sharing. One day it became animal rights, and it was just too perfect because the guy she was dating at the time, Eric, he was the guy who created Protopaste®[8]. *That* guy.

He was really cute, too. But Megan decided she couldn't sleep with a man who committed genocide (on insects). No matter how rich his murders made him.

Megan was always the most intense of our group. I initially saw her as a little out there on the

---

[8] The generic name for the main ingredient in all your insect-based chips, meats, and cheeses.

edge. But she definitely helped me gain a new
perspective on this troubled world we live in.

We got arrested for Mass Disturbance on the
same day. I was frantic and scared. Megan was
calm and sardonic. "You can't blame the PWRS,"
she kept saying. "They're just trying desperately to
cling to all they have left: their illusions of control."

I knew what she meant. Life was getting
difficult for the people at the top.

Business used to be *so* good. Not very long
ago, you probably recall, everything functioned
smoothly. Money was being made at the preferred
rate. The millwheel was churning.

In the boom times, just a decade or so earlier
there were still plenty of drug offenders, gun
offenders, and hackers. Prison was known to be
such a miserable experience (rape laws apparently
do not apply there) that defendants on trial would
threaten to commit suicide if they were sent away. I
remember in my teen years when we had that spate
of prisoner suicides in, like, 2075? Everyone
realized that the system was working perfectly.

Plus, practically speaking, some additional
bed space had opened up and would soon be filled
with another representative from the permanent
underclass. They could barely keep up on the
supply side of cells to meet the incarceration
demand.

That was then. A decade later, in 2084, I remind you, things were different.

With the new Indo-Sino-backed regime and a new Super Supreme Court in place, America was briefly a much nicer place than when I grew up.[9] The average person seemed better off. People were less angry.

Remember when all the druggies were let out and paid restitution for false imprisonment? I think deregulated backyard cannabis was selling for, like, Y$8-a-pound. Best thing: Records were expunged and former "felons" could become part of the workforce. Plunging unemployment = good times.

It all seemed cool, except for what was euphemistically called the "inventory problem." Too *much* inventory.

Prison cells were going empty.

For a while, the authorities made a big deal out of going after unauthorized gene-splicers and other intellectual criminals. But at the time, the "crime" of wind piracy was actually the most-committed offense. It was at an all-time high. Yet, how many wind pirates go to prison?[10] Not many.

---

[9] LOVED the Super Court's slogan: "Making 13 Lucky Again"
[10] Department of Unintended Truth: the parliamentary term "filibuster" is derived from the

So without potheads to incarcerate and the authorities unable (unwilling?) to go after wind pirates, the prison business, the largest growth industry in the United States of the past 100 years was on the brink of collapse. The incarceration industry was desperate for inmates to fill the bunks, desperate to give the union prison guards something to do. Remember?

That's when the trouble started. When they decided to replace criminals with the mentally dangerous.

When they passed the first of the laws against Mass Disturbances in late '83, most of us thought we had a pretty good idea of what "mentally dangerous" meant. We didn't think it meant us!

My generation grew up believing the words of Maeve Bowden, our first lesbian President (and the second Occupy Candidate to win): "In this age of nearly complete corporate control, causing a disturbance, a disruption, is the *only* thing you can do." We were peaceful, but we weren't going to countenance another hurricane in Los Angeles. And we damn sure weren't going to make the same mistakes our parents and grandparents had made.

Dutch word for "pirate." No? Check your arm, fool! #knowsherbizness.

Some very powerful PWRS thought that made us "mentally dangerous."

Fortunately, I never spent a day in jail. Neither did Megan, although we both know a lot of people who did. I'm sure you do, too. My step-brother Daniel, Jr. – the honorable Congressman Huxley; yes, *him* – called whomever he had to call and everything was dismissed quietly.

The whole "mentally dangerous" issue -- there were legal challenges and sorta cool multimedia events made out of it, and I'm pretty sure that if you're able to read this on your arm you're in no danger at this point of getting arrested. Because as you're probably aware (if you've looked at an alert any time in the past five years; *hello*?), they found a *much larger* group to label "mentally dangerous." Suddenly they had more customers than they could handle!

The official link has been disabled, of course. But here's a backdoor approach. Put in "Clive Richter + Alabama State Legislature + family discipline speech + Rkive4ever." That will take you to the shadow vault.

If you don't have that capability – I'm sorry. I don't know what to say. Life is not fair. But if you don't, here it is copied and pasted. #beingofservice.

"The maintenance of civil order in our fragile society rests on a rock solid

foundation of *family discipline*. A child who
disrespects his parents must be removed
from society. Permanently. So that other
children will see the importance of
respecting their parents.

The only political solution left to the
fundamental problems in our society is the
Bible. We must consistently apply God's
higher law to our lower law. Either we're
following God's plan for us or the Devil's.
It's that simple. We do not take the death
penalty lightly. There must be guidelines for
putting children to death. Ours may be found
in Deuteronomy 21:21: 'Then all the men of
his city shall stone him to death with stones;
so you shall put away the evil among you,
and all Israel shall hear and fear.'

Now, this passage does not give parents
blanket authority to kill their children. They
must follow the proper procedure, going to
court and such, laying out their case to the
appropriate judicial authority. Due process,
in the parlance of our troubled times.

There are many rebellious children; there are
few parents resigned or brave enough to take
their children to court and ask them to be put
to death. However, imagine if it were the
law of the land! Such a law would be a
tremendous incentive for poorly behaved

children to obey their parents and give proper respect."

Our economy really turned around when they replaced all the criminals in our prisons with the mentally dangerous. Commerce got good for *everyone*, not just all the people Prison Corp® employs. It's the after-markets, the people who supply and provide support to the core business, people who have jobs indirectly *because* of Prison Corp®. Trickle-down, it's called.

The bad part, of course, is that with most of the crazy superstitious types safely locked up, the National Lottery™ jackpot has shrunk dramatically.

I'm mentioning all this because there was a great big upside. The unintentional but totally fantastic result of the prisoner swap was that *the Termite Squad could happen.*

It could flourish, unhindered at every step in the process by some kooky right-to-life group. With most of those problematic "believers" behind bars, rational adults were able to conduct a mostly civil conversation on the merits of allowing our eldest elders to become volunteer heroes.

Look, all the reliable social metrics are clear: a majority of society (52.4%) is in favor of allowing our Grannies and Grammies and Nanays and Abuelas to die with dignity. And not only dignity but also with a sense of patriotic worth.

Some, the minority of citizens, aren't "comfortable with" the Termite Squad, but I'm not sure exactly what's troubling them. After all these years post-Groningen Protocol, post-Neiblibber Protocol, infanticide isn't really such a dirty word any more. If we can terminate under the age of 12…? Plus, we've been allowing at-home self-determined endings – Final Night™ herbal tea, anyone? -- for decades now.

And for as long as anyone can remember we've assassinated our enemies with a well-aimed drone missile.

With the advent of the Termite Squad, we honor *both* traditions.

As the first woman – the first *person* -- to break the Termite Squad age-barrier, to strap on my Endvest™ with the same sense of purpose as the elders who have gone before me, I feel a sense of abiding contentment. I know my actions will benefit my society and my planet. #atpeacewithmydecision

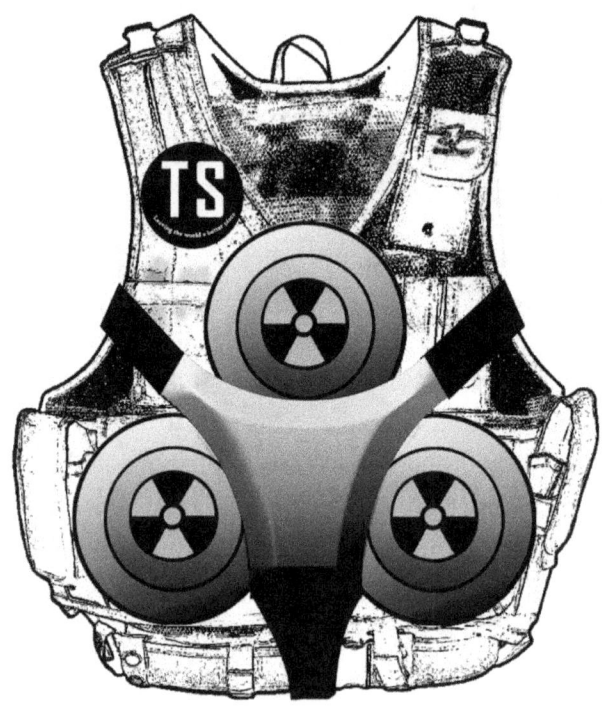

Premonition Vision

I've told myself *there is no pressure. There is no stress.* It's like my mantra.

But now I'm seeing things, vividly, stronger than *déjà vu*. I'm seeing my future.

A tall man, maybe 40-something, emerges from the darkness at the edge of the room. He's wearing a military uniform, cut well and adorned with a mosaic of medals. He has exceptionally blue eyes, exceptionally white teeth, and an exceptionally chiseled jaw. Super handsome, super male. "This is Colonel Flurk," Coach Mike says. "He'll be your mission controller. He's in charge."

"Ms. Galt," the Colonel says, staring in my eyes. "The pleasure is all mine." He extends his hand, the one without the wedding ring.

"Colonel Flurk," I say, staring back at him, placing my little hand in his. He squeezes gently, and then a little more firmly.

He has a flat, Midwestern voice, with like a three-note range. No emotion. "On behalf of the United States of America, I thank you, Ms. Galt, for your selfless service to the men and women of this great country. We are all grateful and humbled by your patriotism."

"We all do what we can, Colonel," I say, smiling my best I've-got-a-secret smile. "Some of us are just lucky to be able to do more than others."

"That's a fine attitude, ma'am," he says. "That's what heroes are made of."

My smile widens, because I really do have a secret. "Each of us has her own definition of 'hero,' Colonel Flurk. I wonder if you'll be telling people I'm a hero once I'm gone."

His eyes flash with annoyance. "Of course I will," he says measuredly. "And so will other proud Americans. They'll be talking about you until the end of their days. And so will their children and grandchildren. You'll always be remembered as a great American hero."

Others Considered

I'm trying to be as blunt about this as possible: I Joan Galt do NOT condone the ongoing operation of the Termite Squad, as presently managed by the CIA.

Everyone – and I mean *everyone*, American, Chinese, Russian, everyone – knows about the Termite Squad. It's no longer a covert operation. It never really was.

Well, maybe it was before Mrs. Edwina Erica Edwards[11]. After she took down Kim-Jong Choi and the Korean nuclear market in '87, the truth gradually came out.

All the posts that have been written about her – we may never know all the details. Mrs. Edwards may or may not have actually been 100,[12]

---

[11] Triple E. #e3hero.

and it may have been pancreatic cancer and not liver – but, really, what's the difference? Kim was Evil. He had to go. And Mrs. Edwards had the honor of taking him with her.

After that, it became increasingly difficult for government officials to claim the Termite Squad didn't exist. And yet, to this day, they *still* don't officially acknowledge it on the record. Like Brazil, refusing to admit they possess an ionizing bomb. Our leaders cling to the charade of "deniability." Their explanation has always been that self-immolating elders were acting unilaterally, without any support or involvement of the U.S. government. When the grannies happen to take out an enemy of the USA – well, that was just pure coincidence.

For some time I sort of believed the official story myself, until I realized that a 100-year-old woman could never lift an Endvest™ without helpers. Way too heavy! LOL

So I guess they'll also call me "traitor" along with all the other names. Whatever. *You* know the Termite Squad exists. *I* know it exists. And so it doesn't really matter what President Patel says, or what the CIA says, or what "allegations" TMZ reports. It's real.

---

[12] "Centurion or Fraud? The Story Behind America's First Martyr," by Pedro Minkster, gives the most details.

And I'm here to tell you that it's screwed up. It's wrong.

Look, I don't think anyone would argue that protecting the world from genocidal madmen like Garcia or Abdul al-Masri is a bad thing. The world is definitely a safer and less murderous place without them. Fewer slaughters.

But I've seen the lists. And, believe me, trust me, the CIA has a *very broad* definition of "Enemy of North America."

The Kill Lists, I'm talking about. I've seen them.

If you're clever, and I know you are because you're reading or scanning this, you're probably thinking, *"Only two people are supposed to know what's on the Termite Squad Kill List: the Director of Operations and the President of the United States of America. Not some girl."*

You would be right. But thanks to my "friendship" with the Director, which Jonah supported completely and even helped arrange sort of in an indirect way, *three* people know what's on the list. And if this gets shared as much as I hope it will, many millions of people more will know.

And I don't think anyone will be too happy about it. #transparencyisabitch

Oh for sure, some Americans will be happy that the Termite Squad is used recklessly. "Kill 'em all!" is their credo. There will always be those who think that the entire world would instantly be a better place if it followed our example and did what it was told. Most of those people own surface-to-air drone-killer missiles and seldom leave their private compound.

The majority, I think, will be as disgusted as I was to discover that the Kill List isn't filled exclusively with the wicked Kim-Jong Chois of the planet. The Kill List is basically anyone we don't like.

And by "we," I mean the President and the Director. Anyone *they* don't like.

Taiwanese hackers who program better computer worms than we do? Philippine bishops who refuse to distribute birth control to their illiterate and destitute congregations? The President of Antigua, for "economic crimes" against our banking system?

Bad guys, sure. But these were not worthy assassination targets. These were not noble missions.

These weren't the kind of deserving victims that would make a grandchild proud of her heroic Nana.

You might wonder, *"Hey, why didn't you try to convince your boyfriend the Director to change his mind? You know men will do anything for* katori *action!"*

First of all, he was not my boyfriend. #disgustingthought.

He was a man with information. It's called trading. A fair exchange.

Second, men *will* do anything for *katori* action – except when they can't. Like when they can't overrule the President of the United States or convince him not to keep a grudge against his political opponents.

I could get the Director to do a lot of things. But editing the Kill List wasn't one of them.

Also, if he knew I'd seen the list I'd probably be dead already. One of the reasons I'm not going to publish this until the very last minute, literally, is because the second I post this document they'll know where I am. And that will be the last you'll hear from me, whether or not my Endvest™ works.

So, sorry everyone in Langley. This is the truth. All other edited versions will contain lies. **The truth is** I saw the Kill List while the Director slept – I saw it *on his arm* while he slept.

Yep. #Assangelives

Gives you great confidence in the people you pay billions to ensure your security, doesn't it? A career CIA man, our nation's top intelligence mind, and it's displayed *on his arm* while he's asleep.

Embarrassing. #truthhurts

Now that I'm revealing our "relationship," he probably wishes I was still alive so he could kill me himself. Too late, I'm afraid. Maybe next time.

It's been very lonely keeping this all to myself. Have you ever kept a secret? Something that you can't ever discuss with anyone, not even your very best friend, not even the love of your life? It eats at you like unresolved rage. It aches inside. You feel no one can fully understand you because they don't know what you know, and *you can never tell them.* You'll always have a secret. You'll always be in a state of solitude.

I actually feel better writing this down, sharing it. I feel cleansed. Lighter.

All this time I couldn't tell Jonah about the Kill List. Even if he promised, even if he said "this will stay in the vault," I knew somehow his Anonymous☺ friends would find out, and then there was no telling what kind of mayhem might have followed.

They can be cool, the Anons. They have a sense of humor. But they can be dicks, too. Like their fricking Property Worm©. I get the joke. It was funny at first, but now that it's infected every text platform on the planet? Not so much. I *know* some of these guys and just like you I curse them under my breath every time their malware forces all the trademark and copyright crap on every single registered business (and some that aren't). *Grrr.*

W-Mart™. Armscreen®. Anonymous☺. #annoying

For the record again, I would like to make perfectly clear that I, Joan Galt, had no knowledge and have no knowledge of Jonah's involvement with Anonymous☺. My understanding is that he has friends in the organization but that he doesn't actively participate in any of their projects – although he's very good with text platforms. And microchips.

But I'm not stupid. I know that when you communicate directly with any of the Anons, nothing you know or have written down somewhere or possibly even think – none of that is safe anymore. In that sense, they're almost as bad as the feds, but they don't have drones.

I couldn't take the chance of the Anons doing something crazy if they found out who was on the Kill List. So, I swear, Jonah never knew. I never told him.

What I said to him was, "The more I know about how the Termite Squad works, the more I think I need to do something about it."

We were vaporizing and tantrasizing, getting completely connected. Both of our arms were switched off. Not mute, *off.*

He nodded and smirked a little and said, "You're smart. You'll do what you can."

I smiled, or at least I tried to. "We all do what we can. I'm just someone who decided that what she can do is *not* nothing."

We both started giggling. Happy times, for sure.

I miss those days. When you laugh for no reason? When you're with the person you feel you're meant to be with, the one you're most closely connected to, as if that person just totally completes you. Like he's your soulmate.

This is my last apology for being romantic. I can't help it. It's in my genes. All of it. The good and the bad, the beautiful and, I guess if you look at it from a certain viewpoint, the quite ugly and horrible.

The closest I ever got to mentioning the contents of the Kill List to my sweetheart of all eternity was in the most hypothetical, cocktail party-pillow talk-feed chatter kind of way. You know, like, "If you were the President, who would *you* put on the Kill List – if such a thing actually existed. Theoretically speaking."

Jonah sort of played along. "That barista on the corner, the one who claims each espresso he steams is an offering from Mother Earth?"

"Seriously. If you had the power to choose."

He shrugged. "Chin, obviously. What is it now? Is it eighty-million now? Of his own countrymen? Like, a twentieth of the population, I think."

"Good one. Yeah. For sure," I mumbled.

"Is it limited to people who commit crimes against humanity?" Jonah mused.

I exhaled long, thinking. "Gotta be," I said. "Otherwise you'd have to assassinate Dellie and, what's that guy? The ones carrying out the animal genocide, the war on mammals and winged creatures."

Jonah chuckled. "You've been interfacing with Megan a lot lately, right?"

Militant Vegans, of course, don't participate in or condone the whole insect-protein model. They think cricket farms are immoral. I once was OIP with my girlfriend Joyce, the nutri-healer. I offered her a totally organic, "sun" baked, fresh bag of

Jiminy Chips™, and she looked aghast, like I was handing her a flame-grilled rodent.

"What's wrong?" I asked. "They're delicious! And studies have shown they make you sexier."[13]

I was so naïve back then. "You're so naïve, Jo," my progressive friend said. "Nothing can make you feel good if it was the product of mass murder."

"Maybe that's true," I said noncommittally. At the time, I felt like laughing. Now, I get it.

Jonah nodded at me. "OK. So just the evilest of the evilest. The pathologically violent dictators and tyrants, right?"

I shouted, "Arms dealers! Weapons makers. They've got to be eligible! Eliminate them, you eliminate a massive amount of suffering. Also, the irony of taking them down with one of their own products…"

"For sure," Jonah replied. "You don't have to be a head-of-state to hurt a lot of people."

---

[13] That *is* what the studies said at the time. People who switched from meat to insects showed an increased attractiveness to potential mates. It hadn't yet been reported that the cricket industry had sponsored the studies.

We both stopped talking. His words sort of hung there for a while.

"Interesting," I said.

"Yes. Interesting. Because if you look at it that way," Jonah said, "maybe the most net good for humanity, for the future of our species, would be to take out Uncle Warren Singh."

We laughed and laughed. And then we took the tantra to another level and I lost interest in theoretical discussions.But the next morning, I did some research

He Shouldn't Be Called Anything Remotely Familiar

We know all his nicknames: The
Stockpicker from Paducah. Warren the Magnificent.
Wise Warren.

And, of course, Uncle Warren.

Good old Uncle Warren. Everyone loves old
Uncle Warren. He's a *sweetheart*. His canasta
parties. His incredible generosity to charities. His
very used, very unspiffy bicycle – the one he rides
to work every day, like any other Joe Lunchbucket.
He's a living oxymoron: the humble multi-
billionaire.

Uncle Warren is a great man. The United
States of America is fortunate to count Mr. Warren
Singh as a taxpaying citizen, the largest among us.
In that way he really is our Uncle, looking after us,

giving us presents every now and then, serving as an excellent role model of what we could have become if only we were slightly more determined.

Uncle Warren Singh. Who owns the company that owns the companies that own our lives. *That* Uncle Warren.

A share in Uncle Warren's business – still based in Kentucky after all these years – costs about Y$2,500,000. Some people slightly below Uncle Warren on the economic food chain own some of the shares, which makes them very, very rich. Uncle Warren owns the rest, which makes him the richest man in the world. By a mile. By almost Y$420 billion more than Hu Xiaopei, the next wealthiest.

Everyone knows his biography. But go ahead and check. You'll see that every single account mentions his childhood poverty, his third-generation immigrant status, working as a housekeeper at his parents' Residence Motel, his averageness in school. His thriftiness. Uncle Warren Singh is a regular guy, a man just like you and me other than he's a trillionaire and we're not.

There's another big difference between Uncle Warren Singh and you: *he's got a special gene*. So, you see, he's not really a member of the family. He's not my uncle. He's not your uncle.

Uncle Warren Singh is another species.

Your Tax Dollars at Work

After what they did to all the great leakers in history – your Edward Snowdens, your Damon Delfts, your Mike Dombrowskis – it's no wonder that so much of the really amazing and fascinating and slightly unbelievable stuff that our government does goes unnoticed (or unrecognized) by the American public.

I can't put it more simply: *there's lots of stuff they don't want you to know about.*

The Termite Squad? Official denials notwithstanding, they *wanted* you and the rest of the world to know about it, even if it was "secret." Otherwise, absent a brave leak martyr, you wouldn't have heard about it.

That's pretty much the way things work. If they want you to know about it, you will. If they don't, you won't. They're very good at controlling their messaging.

You'll never know about some of the incredible experiments being carried out at the CIA unless someone on the inside, someone with clearance and access, is brave enough to be a leaker, courageous enough to face torture and a life sentence in solitary confinement.

I'm not claiming to be brave or courageous. In fact, I'm probably the opposite. But after I post this, what are they going to be able to do to me? Put my remains on trial? #sadthought.

I confess that I have precious little documentation to share with WikiLeaks or the Anons. What memos and experiment logs I was able to copy will be posted with those networks simultaneous with the publication of this report. (How secure their servers will be in the aftermath, I can't say.) But even the few things I was able to rip will give you some insight into what your tax dollars are paying for at the moment.

And I just want to clarify: I didn't originally join the CIA out of any sense of patriotism or whatever. I needed a job in D.C. to be near my man. I wanted that job to pay decently and challenge my brain and use some of the otherwise useless skills I learned at The Harvard™. A junior analyst position at the CIA was the best my step-brother the honorable Congressman Daniel Huxley, Jr., could arrange.

For a young politician, he's very plugged-in at the Agency, thanks to his dad, my step-father the Senator. His connections are what got me on the inside. I wrote him a nice thank you letter – an actual email. I copied Elaine on it. He sent me back a two-word TexThought®: **Ur wlcme.**

I think he was just glad to have the bothersome step-sister out of what's left of his hair.

After I passed all the background checks and psychological evaluations (funny!), they gave me an office, a very small office, without a window. Since I was expected to be peering into monitors, a view was considered superfluous. The office was unremarkable in every way except for one thing: it was on the same floor, on the same hallway, as a number of fascinating projects.

Some of them are sort of cute. My friend Cassandra -- who is the sweetest girl and **has no knowledge whatsoever of Termite Squad operations**. I would like to emphasize that. We knew each other a little at The Harvard™, but not besties or anything. At the Agency, Cassandra worked in the culinary wing, where they were always figuring out stuff to do to food. Poisons, paralyzers, I guess. I didn't ask and she didn't tell.

One evening we were tube-pooling home together (with Jeff and Joel; more on them later). Cassandra sometimes handed out little "treats" during the quad-pod ride.

"Try this," she said, handing out little geodesic pellets, the size of a soybean. They were white and chalky.

"And this would be?" Jeff asked.

"Candy," Cassandra said. "Seriously excellent candy." And she ate one.

I ate one. It was a little dry, but quite sweet, in a cool minty way. Nothing amazing, but nice.

The boys ate theirs. "Breath freshener. Good. Very good," Joel said.

"You guys tell me if you notice anything later tonight," Cassandra said.

"Something bad?" I said, maybe a little too alarmed. Cassandra had never done us wrong before.

"No. Something good!"

That night, before bed, I used the bathroom. Can I just tell you that when I was finished the whole house smelled like tangerines?

I'm not talking about one strong smell masking another strong smell. I'm talking about one uniform delicious and citrusy aroma, coming from my waterless toilet.

I sent Cassandra a TexThought®. "WTF? I'm living in an orange grove!"

She replied, "Jeff got the rose flavor."

The next morning, we're in the tube to Langley, and we're all, "Cassandra, you got some *splaining* to do, girl!"

"We call them feces fresheners. And they definitely work," Cassandra said. "But the practicality –"

Joel interjected, "What's the application – why?"

"I'm not sure," Cassandra said, shrugging. "I heard something about paving the way for more aboveground sewers. Like, if we can make Bamako and Kinshasa –

We all noticed it right away. "Jeff! Yow!" If there was a window I would have rolled it down. The smell was overwhelming. The entire quad-pod smelled like fresh roses.

"Still tweaking dosages," Cassandra said, with a squinting grin.

But I don't want to give the impression that everything going on at the Agency was light-hearted and silly. When you're part of a team that goes to work every morning convinced that you're saving what little is left of the free world, the mood is somber and the focus intense. People do their jobs. No one laughs. Calling attention to yourself or your project is considered poor manners, and it's potentially dangerous.

Information – *intelligence* – is the currency. You learn quickly to hoard it (like everything else in this world) or else you lose it to someone else, and when you lose it you have nothing. You're not useful anymore. So people keep quiet.

Those that don't keep quiet pay the price. I remember this guy Doug, former military, former Wall Street. High-achiever dude. He had a TwitLord™ rating and the insatiable habit that goes with it. Couldn't stop himself. One evening he wrote: "Did you know that cancer causes jobs? #truth."

His post seemed innocuous. But, later it was revealed that "Cancer Causes Jobs" was the name of the project Doug was working on at Langley. An "economic assassination project" I think they called it. The next morning Doug didn't arrive at his office. And that was the last anyone ever heard from him. His feed remained "active" but untouched for another few days, until someone remembered to turn it off.

The Agency is a serious place. Serious people. *Smart* people. The kind of super-brainy people Jonah loves to hang with. But unlike the hackers and the performance artists who used to breeze in and out of our lives, Agency people aren't really the kind you'd want to be friends with. They (we, I guess) always have secrets. They can never be totally real.

Maybe that's why I never fit in there. I mean, I got along with my fellow commuters and with the colleagues I saw in the cafeteria and with all the people up the food chain. I liked them from all my online accounts, I pumped up their totals. But I can't say I was friends[14]. I wouldn't meet them OIP voluntarily.

The Director? I was very friendly with him.

I'm sure the share numbers for this report would spike if I made up some incredible story about sneaking through secret CIA passageways while being strapped to a ticking nuclear mini-bomb, or something. But the truth isn't that exciting, I'm afraid. Just like with the Kill Lists, I saw what I'm about to tell you *on his arm*. While he slept.

Very low tech espionage. Ridiculous, actually. But it worked.

[14] Except maybe for one other person, whose name I don't want to use for this person's protection.

This is how I came to know about what the popular media are now calling "splicers." Gene mappers, gene designers. DNA-jockeys (or "DJ"s). Even then, in 2089, every major university and research hospital had a splicing center. Ours, which wasn't located in Langley, but which we controlled, was taking the splicing game to a whole new level.

Ours was in a small shopping center in Maryland. While the hospitals were figuring out how to use the gene maps to eradicate muscular dystrophy and spina bifida, we – your public servants – were figuring out how to manufacture the next super species fighting machine, the iHuman.

I know. It's not like the biggest surprise ever, considering that the majority of us in the civilized world, those who can afford it anyway, have already had our screens implanted and integrated with our flesh. Pundits have been predicting a "next step" for years. Despite all the official denials from Washington, Bejing and Mumbai, most people I know figured this was going on somewhere, in secret.

They were right.

What they don't know is that all this work on the next generation human has accidentally produced some shocking discoveries.

Where it Gets Complicated

So I'm having a candle sim with Jonah. All our feeds are turned off. We're vaporizing. We're tantrasizing. We're connecting. It's perfect.

I'm talking dirty. I'm telling Jonah what I would do to a cute girl, a cute virgin girl, if he was allowed to watch. He likes when I talk like this. He *begs* me to talk like this. I'm not ashamed. I'm totally comfortable. I feel good. I feel sexy. And strong. And *powerful*. I'm not afraid and I'm not ashamed. I'm Joan Galt.

"And would she moan?" he asks, longingly.

"Mmm. Oh, yes, she would. She might even cry out."

"From pain or pleasure?"

"Both," I say, biting his lower lip.

You can figure out where this is all headed – where it was supposed to be headed. And it would have if Jonah hadn't mentioned Marcy.

"I've got the perfect girl for you," he said. "Just the kind you like."

"Oh, yes?"

He began to describe this perfect girl: tall, athletic, firm body, shy energy, innocent-seeming, with a manly haircut, name of Marcy.

"You would love Marcy," he predicted. "And she would love you, I'm sure."

"Jonah," I said, slightly annoyed. "Is this, like, a real woman. She exists?"

He sensed this was not cool. "Yes. Is that bad?"

"So you know her? She's a friend?"

"Well, yes, I think *friendly* is maybe more accurate."

I explained to him that the whole fantasy thing didn't work for me when it was a friend of his. An actual acquaintance.

"She's not my *current* friend," Jonah explained. "She's an ex."

That was the end of the tantrasizing for that evening.

As with many things in this strange world, Jonah was right: I *would* like Marcy. I ended up liking her a lot.

Turns out they had hooked up briefly – for maybe two months? – when Jonah first moved to Washington from New York. They had known each other at online school, via videoconferencing, but hadn't had an in-person contact until later, which probably increased their attraction totals once they met outdoors. Jonah was just getting started with his progressive organizing work and Marcy was already toiling in a private laboratory doing things with DNA that she wasn't allowed to discuss with him.

I could see why he would be attracted to her: she's super brilliant. I think that gives a woman – well, anyone, really, but especially a woman – it gives her the kind of quiet confidence that people instinctively want to be near.

At least I did. After I got past the fact that the love of my life, my Jonah, had tantrasized with this intensely attractive woman, I started to see what it was about Marcy that drew him to her. She wasn't beautiful, yet she was irresistible somehow, her otherness. Magnetic.

He introduced us. We immediately liked each other. We became friends.

And eventually we met outdoors, in person.
#OIP

How can I say this? I knew from the start
that Marcy was bisexual, and I'm sure she could
sense that I am, too, even though I don't wear my
hair in a butch cut.[15] But at the start of our
relationship, we never did anything together, not
even flirty messaging. We never even discussed
anything like that. Maybe out of respect to Jonah? I
don't know. We just didn't go there. That seemed
like the smartest and most responsible thing to do.

In retrospect, I think having an underlying
current of attraction between us created an
interesting energy, a sort of tension-and-release, but
without the release. You know, a shared smile? An
eye-lock that lasts just a little too long? It's a
curiosity that's never satisfied. Sometimes I'd get a
little flash of attraction to Marcy from something
she said, or her incredibly cute lack of fashion sense
that somehow improbably *worked*. I said nothing,
but I suspected she could tell what I was thinking.

What we *did* talk about was all the stuff girls
supposedly never talk about because they're too
busy talking about clothes and boys and the
questionable choices made by other girls who may
or may not be their friend. We talked about *the
world*.

---

[15] More of a punk-meets-glam cut.

Marcy, let me just say, is one of those people whose smartness can almost be intimidating. *She's* not intimidating; she's a sweetheart. But Marcy's mind? Scary.

The first time we met OIP, at The Coffee Store™, after dispensing with niceties about moving to DC and what a great guy Jonah was and what a small world it was, I asked Marcy why she did what she did – gene splicing, life engineering. "You seem like you could do anything. Why this?"

She smiled, as though she'd heard this question before. I expected she would be all scientific. Devoted to evolution and such. The pursuit of Truth.

"Can I tell you a story, Joan?" she asked.

"Sure," I said. "I love stories."

"Good. Me, too. So, after many years in seclusion, the greatest artist of his time finally granted an interview to a news portal. Have you heard this one?"

"I don't think so," I said. I wanted to hear her tell it.

Marcy continued. "So, the reporter sent to the artist's studio had been instructed to get the insider secrets, the facts. The truth about how the artist makes his art. When the two met, standing beside one of the artist's famous trash sculptures, those heaps towering toward the ceiling, the reporter asked his first question: 'Why did you make this sculpture?' The artist looked at the trash heap, thought for a second, shrugged, and finally said, 'Because I'm the only one who can.' After that, there were no more questions."

I understood what Jonah saw in this girl. I hit mute right before my Connection Alerts® would have started buzzing like a vibrator lying on loose change. "Cool," I said, probably not as coolly as I intended. "I get it. I think."

Marcy nodded. "I'm not saying there's nobody in the whole wide world who can do what I'm doing with the human genome. I'm saying I'm the only one right now currently doing what I do. Does that make sense?"

"It does," I said. "I think it does."

On the tubular ride home, I thought about how assured Marcy seemed. She wasn't swaggering and arrogant. She wasn't boastful. She was just very certain, very sure.

Up until this day, this very day, I don't think I've ever been very sure of anything. Having an "unorthodox" childhood will do that to you.

As the pod settled into the station, I caught my reflection in the window across from my seat. I saw a pretty woman. I saw a smart woman. I saw someone I might like. But I didn't see a person who did something because *she was the only one who could.*

I didn't see an artist.

What I saw was someone who might improve humanity by being a Termite.

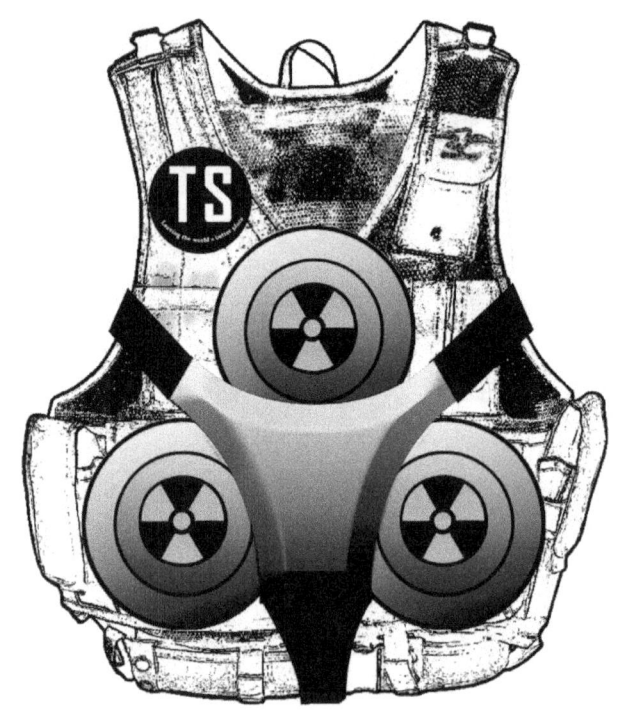

Etymology and Entomology

There's a long-running (and boring) editing war on Wiki involving the origins of the Termite Squad. Does it really matter what the "philosophical source material" was for the project? Even with all the searchable databases, when it comes to really big ideas, it's still sort of impossible for anyone, scholars included, to identify *the very first person* to have a thought.

So we can't really say for certain who was the "father" or "mother" of the movement. We can't even say who was the first to think of applying *termite strategy* to foreign affairs.

For me it's like the ongoing Shakespeare argument. Does it really matter who wrote them? What matters is that they were written at all[16].

---

[16]If you like difficult-to-read-and-understand poetry

The revisionists have their theories about who deserves the credit: Professor Stefan Balaby, former Secretary of State (and MankindCorp® CEO Louis Turkee), the media guru Paul Glurnered. All these guys have merits. They moved the termite discussion forward and deserve partial credit.

But I'm with the originalists. I think *termite strategy*, or "the termite method," can be traced to an essay written by an amateur etymologist named Michael Smalpuni, published way back in 2013 on IrreverentInsectInsights.org, a Website dedicated to observing insects (not eating them). It was officially called "Something We Can Learn from Termites," but most people just call it the "Smalpuni Essay," or if you're an academic, just "Smalpuni."

Assuming something really weird doesn't happen between the time I finish writing this and posting it, the link for Smalpuni's essay should still be active. But just in case they disabled it…I'm pasting the most important part.

> …Then, through the transparent cut-out, I'm able to see a virtual cross-section of the termite nest beneath my house. These are fascinating creatures, with amusing antics, especially around egg-laying time.
>
> One trait stands out. I'm sure scientists have previously discovered this, although I have not found much literature on it. What I noticed: Certain termite species send their elderly - male and female - on

of the ancient times.

suicide missions. They literally blow themselves up through the abdomen. These toxic explosions harden and serve to block invaders from conquering the nest. The deaths have a great utility. The elderly termites always seem to know where to explode themselves, the place where their remains will best protect the home turf.

The termites I observed go a step beyond what used to be called the Eskimo Way, which involved the elderly voluntarily leaving the igloo and ending their life alone on an ice floe. In the Termite Method, not only does the nest rid itself of unwanted old workers, but there seems to be a kind of selflessness at work here. As the termites end their life, they somehow understand that they're leaving the world a better and safer place for their fellow termites.

The concept was batted around rhetorically for a few decades, run through a kind of Web refinery, until, all of a sudden, it's 2080 and you can start finding Termite Method chat rooms filled with smart (but sort of strange?) netizens arguing quite passionately about sending our Grandmothers on suicide missions.

I may have joined one or two of these groups.

What I found most interesting about the "debate," if you can call anything that occurs in a chat forum such a civilized word, was that almost no one had any problem with using the Termite Method to accomplish our foreign policy goals. *That* was cool. What bugged people was the "euthanasia" aspect.

Was it right to "sacrifice" our elders this way? Did they truly understand what they were signing up for? Would it be morally acceptable to assign termite duty to a granny with dementia?

The ultimate answer to every one of these questions seemed to be: "They're terminal. They're going to die anyway. As long as it's their voluntary choice…"

I feel like I need to emphasize that even, like, 10-15 years ago, the national mindset was not the way it is today. Back then, you may recall, the elderly had the legal right to quasi-manage their death. But they had no *support*. No government-supplied suicide kit. No familial encouragement to go earlier than later. No dignity. No *status*.

It must have been awful to be a Centurion. Then, slowly at first and then a little faster and then quickly, the way these things always seem to go, I remember there being a lot of positive talk about termites.

The national mood seemed to shift to: "Hey, they would be wasting away in expensive nursing facilities. This way they can be heroes and we'll build statues of them."

Today, it's a hot thing. It's a fashion statement.

Not judging, but I think Termite Squad t-shirts and caps are a bit much. I get it: Progressive movements need positive imagery.[17] Speaking from very personal experience, I can assure you that

---

[17] Like Occupy's "I'll Be Here for Eternity" Buddha merchandise.

nobody joins the Termite Squad looking for monetary rewards – although, yes, absolutely, the ample (but not extravagant) annuity provided to the deceased's designated heir gives some peace of mind.

Not that anyone I know will ever see one Yuan-Dollar. They don't pay out to girls who break the rules.

Premonition Vision 2

I see it all so clearly. I must be jumping dimensions, slipping through a black hole, coming out the other side.

"Termite Joan, your dress," Melanie says, handing me the chic evening frock that I've already started thinking of as "my little black dress," as if it's my go-to choice for a night on the town. It really is fabulous.

I take it from her. She motions toward a screened –off changing area, where I presume the tub was situated previous to sacrificing itself for Termite Squad service. I step behind the screen, which the assistant closes behind me.

I start to remove my sweatshirt. "Dylan? Mission Control?"

I hear Dylan clear his throat. "Yes?"

"Can you see me right now?"

"You mean..."

"Can you see me changing?"

"You're in full view. Yes. For your own protection."

"OK." I remove my clothes, telling myself I'm doing a good thing. For my community. For my sisters and brothers. I don't let myself think about the eyes on my naked skin. I can't. I have a mission to accomplish.

One of My Lunches with Elaine

Do I have issues with my birth mother Elaine Huxley?

Yes. Sure. Of course I do. Don't we all have *something* with our mother?

It would be incorrect, however, to give the impression that I blame Elaine for anything.

Let me be super clear: I do not blame Elaine for *anything*. We all do what we have to do. We all do what we can.

I'm me. I make my own decisions. My birth mother has no effect on those decisions. I'm cool with Elaine and I assume she's cool with me up to a point, after which she's definitely *not* cool with me. But that's just the way it is.

I consider her more of an older (and still beautiful) friend than a relation. Soon you might say she *was* my gal pal. For now, I can say she *is* my gal pal. My gal pal Elaine (who happened to deliver me from her uterus).

We started having a semi-regular outdoors gal pal lunch every few months. Elaine would text me one word: **Lunch?**

Me: **OK. When?**

It was usually one week later, at the same place, Kai & Goh's Pipe Dream, a café that freely accommodated vegans and insectivores alike. Elaine would usually bring me something demure – an antique tea cup, an antique pen, sometimes an actual antique book – and made a conscious effort to be non-judgmental, non-bossy. Non-motherly. More like a bff.

We mostly talked about me. Me and Jonah. Me and my work. It was always awkward. There wasn't much I was allowed to say. Sometimes she would ask about the Theo *accumulation* she'd given me. Was it on display? Did people like it? I assured her yes and yes – it was on the wall facing the front door. Unmissable.

Then we would talk about my birth father Theo, until I changed the subject.

At one of these lunches, last year, I asked Elaine if I could record her for my friend Grant's audio-collage installation he was creating for China Bank™ – the same organization managed by her charming brothers, the ones who don't acknowledge my existence. "It's good for everyone," I said, curtailing further explanation.

I set my arm to capture mode. "So, Elaine, this is your daughter Joan. I'm recording this interview for my friend Grant Neckles, and also for my own amusement."

A lot of what we talked about is silly. The part that I'm copying here is important because I remember listening to Elaine say something and feeling – *bam!* -- at that moment that I knew what I had to do! If I had to pinpoint the exact instant when I was like, "*Yes. I see,*" this was it.

After some questions about what life was like right around the time I was born, in 2062, we had gotten onto a general discussion of America: then and now. The differences she'd seen in her lifetime. The path we seemed to be headed on.

Instead of paraphrasing, here's a partial transcription, which I took (without permission; #whatever) from the hard-drive of my implant.[18]

> ME: ...and as a representative of the younger generation, I thank you for sharing the perspective of an older, you know, and wiser demographic.

> ELAINE: I'm glad your professor asked you to do this project.

> ME: He's my friend. He's an artist. Not a...Grant does mostly audio.

> ELAINE: That's wonderful, darling. I'm glad you're talking to a representative of the post-plague generation. My generation. Folks like me know what America was like back then...The USA was different.

> ME: Ya?

---

[18] This is all easy to authenticate. Please do.

ELAINE: How do I mean? Well, I'll tell you. [*clears throat*]. Even in 2040, which isn't really that long ago in the grand scheme, America was still a mean-spirited country. This century. *Progressive* was a dirty word.

ME: Ha!

ELAINE: You know, Joanie, we still had a surprising – and, you know, you could almost call them frightening. Yes. Many people whose beliefs you younger ones would find...archaic. Or despicable, depending on how polite you want to be.

ME: Like what?

ELAINE: Well...[*laughs*]. Before it widely understood that people who identified themselves as Christians were mentally dangerous, a large part of the population actually believed that homosexuals shouldn't have the same rights as heterosexuals.

ME: I don't get it.

ELAINE: Oh, yes. There were even big companies that got involved, trying to get legislation passed to outlaw marriages. Adult marriages, I mean.

ME: Between adults?

ELAINE: Those companies are all out of business now, of course. But back then if you hated gay people you expressed your prejudices by spending your money at gay-hating businesses. Some chicken restaurant got into politics, I think. Oh, yes! They felt that they had to take a position and stand up for God, you know, because His omniscience wasn't what it used to be. Sorry, I can't recall their name today. But I'm sure you can look it up on the eyepiece thing you're always wearing. The iris screen. That thing.

ME: It's turned off.

ELAINE: And speaking of chickens, here's another fact: Back then – you're not going to believe this, Joanie – people still accepted food that was factory produced. Oh, yes. I'm not kidding!

ME: So unappetizing. All the –

ELAINE: With the antibiotics and the feces and the cruelty. And vegetables – oh, this is funny. Do you know that they used to label food "organic"?

ME: No.

ELAINE: Yes, they did!

ME: You would think they'd do the opposite. You know, like now. You label the stuff with cancer-causing chemicals "inorganic."

ELAINE: Of course. Back then they just put labels on properly cultivated food and charged twice as much for it. Do you understand? You actually paid twice as much for the kind of food we all eat today. Back in '50, you could still get cancer-causing foods *cheap*, without any of the excise taxes – we used to call them "sin taxes" when it was cigarettes and alcohol. And believe me...[*laughs*] We were *fat*. I mean fat! Like morbidly obese.

ME: Elaine, I've probably seen every picture of you on the Web and I can't remember a single one where you looked anything close to fat.

ELAINE: Oh, well, *I* wasn't fat. I'm speaking generally. America in general. Not a few, you know, circus freaks. I mean most Americans. I'm sure you've seen the images. Sad. But also sort of funny, too, right? The self-poisoning thing?

ME: How do you mean?

ELAINE: Honey, we knew what corn syrup and sugar and animal fat did to the blood. We knew. It wasn't a secret. But we kept poisoning ourselves anyway. And I'm not sure why. [*inhales deeply*] And...as you well know...since it's only been...How many years since the plague?...[*sighs*] Fate can be cruel. But so can humans.

ME: Sure, there's still cruelty built into our modern world. But my generation believes we're capable of getting hip.

ELAINE: Getting *conscious*. I think that's what Theo, what your father called it.

ME: Yes. Optimism! I believe in evolution. I believe things can change.

ELAINE: Oh, yes, that's possible some times. We just like to take our time about it. Joanie, do you know that – and this a decided and locked subject on Wiki. This is a fact: We used to allow corporations to pollute our water and air and not pay for it. Did you know that?

ME: I did. Yeah.

ELAINE: "Environmentalist" was a term of derision. People accepted poison in their air and water because they'd been conditioned to think about low prices instead of their children and grand-children.

ME: The corporations *still* don't pay their fair share for the pollution they pump into –

ELAINE: It continues to this day! You've still got your climate change deniers—

ME: Well—

ELAINE: And your radical free-marketeers, your little cults of ignorance. But back in '50, there were more of them than you might imagine. [*chuckles*] My generation! Embarrassing.

My generation. Embarrassing.

I didn't want to buzzkill our nice lunch, so I didn't say it out loud. But I was thinking, "You think *you're* embarrassed about *your* generation?"

It's 2090, on the cusp of the 22nd century, and my generation is at war with itself. It's always Us versus Them, a battle pitting people like me and Jonah (and probably *you* if you're still reading this incredibly long post) against people who want things to stay the way they are.

Evolvers versus freezers.

Progress versus greed is what it boils down to. Meaning: People who actively suppress change, who actively stymie the worldwide impulse toward social justice, are usually quite happy with the way things are. Who wants to change when you're rich? When you're ahead? When you've *won*?

I had a big argument once with my friend Megan the Vegan. Not "big" in volume or meanness. Big as in "major philosophical difference."

I was telling her like what I just said: that we as a society don't really truly want to educate *everyone* excellently, that the elites require servants and people to clean up after them. "The system keeps every person in her place."

"That sounds very judgmental," Megan said, narrowing her eyes. We were at her apartment, near the Cambodian Embassy. "Every person finds the place she wants to be. We all create our own happiness."

"Judgmental of people who are victimized by a foul system?"

"Some people are very happy cleaning toilets forty hours a week," Megan said, shrugging, like, "Everyone knows that!"

I said, "I'm sure there are. But I also think it's true that for the vast majority of human beings scrubbing toilets, it wasn't their first choice, their dream. They do it – maybe even happily – because they *have to*."

Megan scrunched up her face. "They don't *have* to. They choose to!"

"OK. But it's probably never anyone's ideal situation."

"Again, Jo, that sounds judgmental. Like you're looking down on people who do manual labor. Servants."

I smiled. Megan was right. I was being judgmental. But she had it backwards.

I looked her in the eye and calmly informed her, "The people who do the actual work aren't the ones I'm looking down on."

HOW SHIT WORKS

Can I simplify things? There are whole books, 100-pagers, devoted to the subject of our monetary system. About how it actually works. Lots of details. I'll just boil it down to the main points.

And let me just say that I give Jonah a lot of credit for exposing me to knowledge, for connecting me with smart people who think we can do better. I learned a lot from him and his friends. However, that does NOT make him responsible.

OK. Money, as you're probably aware, does not exist. Like many other "things" in our modern world, money is a "virtual" commodity. We all agree to assign this virtual commodity a value, but that value is utterly arbitrary and tied to nothing.[19]

Since all the world's major banks, including China Bank™ and Bank of North America™, loan exponentially more money than they have on

---

[19] Nothing except our collective fear of not believing the myth.

deposit, it's theoretically impossible to repay the world's outstanding debt to the banks. There isn't enough money in the overall supply to cover the principal and interest.

Where does the additional money supply come from? Our imagination. How does the money supply constantly grow? Because we print more money.

The banks print money, worth nothing, backed by nothing, except we collectively agree to say that it's worth something. They loan imaginary money and have real money (including foreclosed property and interest) repaid to them. When debtors can't pay – as we've seen recently with Algeria, Portugal, and Belgium – the banks seize all the hard assets, the buildings and the infrastructure, and turn the debtor citizens into indentured servants.

Look at the tallest buildings in your city. Look at the names on the side of the buildings: Banks, insurance companies, accounting firms. The big money is in money. You trade a fictional commodity and end up owning very real property, known as *real* estate. You own everything and everyone.

Some call it organized crime. Some call it the American Way.

To quote Morris Marley III, "that's how shit works." It sucks for most people. But when you're one of my uncles, it's all quite magical!

The Ballad of Jason and George Barclay

I was inspired by MM III's song "Lucky Bruddas." Using that melody – "sing along, yo, sing along" -- I wrote alternate lyrics about my dear uncles, two wonderful fellows who wish I was never born.

Oh, what a glorious life my uncles have had!

Born to the manor these two fine brothers,

Whose servants sheltered them from feeling sad,

Or foolishly acting too kindly to others.

Natural twins from the start, they twinned all through life,

The Harvard™ and clerkships and China Bank™.

Jason got married; George needed a wife

To double the wedding and stay equal in rank.

The Termite Squad:
My Official and Authentic Report

Being a Barclay is grand, oh so grand!
Being a Barclay – well, you can't understand.

How Georgie and Jason achieved to the utmost!
Their lust subject to polite conjecture:
Jetting to Spain, enjoying a slut host,
Eager to hear the twins' austerity lectures?

With work and connections they hatched a large fortune
To add to the one they already had.
More loot to the pile! Ask, importune,
Whine, beg: All for investors in Islamabad.

Each boy has his plane, and girls, as well as a boat,
Mansion in Cabo, vineyard in Bordeaux,
A thoroughbred horse, an alpaca goat
Possessed for the purpose of conspicuous show.

Being a Barclay is grand, oh so grand!
Being a Barclay – well, you can't understand.

The Termite Squad:
My Official and Authentic Report

Now that Jason is a Prez and George is a Vice

They manage a bank that owns half the globe,

Investing in nations naughty and nice –

Oblivious twins missing bits of frontal lobe.

How could they know they carry a noxious disease

Deeply embedded in genetic code?

How could they live and not do as they please?

Sharing (or caring) was never their default mode.

A sick brain at work is what this song is about,

A mind that's made up on all the key points.

An outlook devoid of worry or doubt.

As inflexible and stiff as arthritic joints.

Oh, yes, now strong medicine is coming their way

They're going to get the miracle cure

Bid farewell, Jason and Georgie Barclay

To help us make our world sufficiently pure

How I Got "Radicalized"

What changed me from a nice girl to a monster? I mean, that's what all the investigators will be trying to explain. How could she think such horrible thoughts? Surely she's being controlled by an Imam or a Guru. *Someone* brainwashed her.

I'll save everyone the trouble: there's no conspiracy here.

All that happened was I awoke from a long sleep. I was awakened. Eyes opened.

Have I viewed unauthorized documents? Yes, obviously.

Have I shared unauthorized documents? Yes, and I will continue to do so until I no longer can.

Is anyone compelling me to do any of this? No.

The only thing that drives me is the Truth.

Go ahead and review my Web history. I'm
sure it's already been publicly posted by now.
You'll see that in addition to all the usual stuff –
yes, I like submissive Asian girls! #scandalous –
I've viewed one Banned Video hundreds and
hundreds of times. Like, on an almost daily basis
since 2089. Regularly.

First, can I just say: almost everyone I know
watches Banned Videos, just like almost everyone
breaks traffic laws and calorie laws. So can we get
over it? Everyone knows how to find them. Even
kids.

My high view-count BV, came from very
early in this millennium, like right at the turn of the
century, around 2002. It's a Truthteller Rant.

I don't have time to argue cultural theory
with those who despise Truthtellers. I just want to
say that it's a big mistake to put them in the same
category as Blackface Minstrels, Hardcore Punks,
or any other once-popular and now-discredited
performing art form. I reject the idea that they were
somehow "a product of their time." That's
ludicrous. What they were declaiming nearly 100
years ago is still totally relevant today. These guys
may have been "edgy" or "provocative," but there's
no way you can say that they're anachronisms.

The standard history – at least the one I was
taught – is that in the 20th Century these kind of
public speakers were known as "comedians." They
told funny stories and jokes. They made people
laugh. Think of them as a kind of talented fool, a
clown to amuse the public. With the advent of the
Internet and transparency and all that, information
began to flow freely, and as it did these funny

talkers began to spice their monologues with daring little bits of honesty. They still got laughs, but they also earned a reputation for saying things regular folks weren't able to.

They said out loud what many people were thinking. They weren't afraid. They didn't worry about being popular. They just told the truth. Out loud. Without fear.

Truthteller Rant? The generally accepted reason this new breed of comedian came to be known as a Truthteller was because at their performances audiences would frequently shout out, "Speak the truth! Tell the truth!" in between bouts of laughter.

Standard history also says that gradually their ranting was found to be un-amusing and unhelpful by the targets of their rants, the PWRS. The Truthtellers were accused of being "valueless" to society and legislated into a state of permanent banishment.

For saying things. In public. With video cameras watching them.

That's the great thing about videos: You can ban them, but you can't really destroy them. They always turn up somewhere if you know where to find them…

//4kive4vr.gcLiLV02TR

I understand that I come from a world of privilege that not all my brothers and sisters enjoy. So if you don't have cross-link capabilities, I think that's a shame, a crime, actually. Consider this rough transcription – I used the free downloadable version of Sound2Word™ -- my way of making things easy on you. And on anyone who's looking for "clues" to my state of mind.

Where this was filmed exactly I can't say. Based on the language (English) and look (affluent), most people assume it was shot in an American theater, in front of a potentially dangerous/over-the-congregation-limit audience. The identity of the Truthteller ranting here has been scrubbed by the authorities, but based on his short beard, blue eyes, gravelly voice, and receding hairline, most historians think it's a 20th Century zealot named Eddie Glass, a former comedian/clown who had his home stolen from him during one those early-century property seizures orchestrated by the banks. Before they were nationalized.

The Wiki says Eddie Glass used to do jokes about Hollywood movies, The Coffee Store™, and celebrity weight loss – the standard concerns of the slave-owner class. "Then," it says, "he was radicalized by a forced bankruptcy and newly restrictive speech laws."

Please watch the video (if you're able to without prosecution). You can tell he's pissed. Genuinely.

Is it funny? That's a matter of taste. Is it relevant? To me, what he's talking about 100 years ago might as well be today.

The link again: //4kive4vr.gcLiLV02TR

[applause and laughter]…No, no. There's a reason for all this. There's a reason public education is broken and won't ever be fixed. Why it won't ever get any better. Because the PWRS, the owners of this country, don't want that.

I'm talking about the *real* owners.

I'm not talking about politicians. The politicians are there to play their part – which is to give you the idea that you have freedom of choice. You don't! You have no choice. You have owners.

They own you. They own everything.

They own all the important land.

They own the corporations.

They own the senate, the congress, the state houses, the city halls, the judges.

They own all the big media companies and control most of the news and information you get in your feeds.

The PWRS spend billions of dollars every year lobbying to get what they want. And what they want is more for themselves and less for everybody else.

But there's one thing they *don't* want. They don't want a population of citizens capable of critical thinking. They don't want well informed, well educated people capable of figuring out what's going on. Critical thinking is unhelpful to the PWRS; it's antithetical to their interests.

The PWRS don't want people who are smart enough to figure out how badly they're being exploited by their foul system. They don't want that.

You know what they want? They want obedient workers, people who are just smart enough to run the machines and do the paperwork. People who are intellectually docile enough to accept their horrible job, to accept increasingly lower pay, longer hours, reduced benefits, and a vanishing pension.

Your retirement money? The money you earned from a lifetime of labor? They want that, too. The PWRS want it so they can "redistribute" it to their criminal friends.

You know they'll get it. They'll get it *all* sooner or later. Because, really, *it's theirs*. They own the world. It's a big world but it's a small club – and you and I aren't in it.

You and I will never be members of this Mafia.

The only "club" involving you is the figurative one they use to beat you over the head, clubbing you with propaganda. They beat you into believing exactly what they tell you to believe. The media – *their* media – clubs you into submission, telling you what to believe, what to think, and what to buy.

This isn't a fair game. It's rigged.

And few of us seem to notice. Even fewer seem to care. Good people, honest people, hardworking people – people of relatively modest means compared to the PWRS – these regular people continue to elect greedy narcissists who don't care about them.

I'll say it again – and they'll probably torture me for it: The PWRS don't care about you, no more than they do a cage of crickets. They don't care about you at all.

But so long as everyone pretends that they do, we can all get along. The revolution can wait. The revolution gets postponed. Because we convince ourselves that our masters care about us.

The owners of this world sleep better at night knowing that the average person will remain willfully ignorant of their exploitation. The owners of this world know the truth: it's called "the American dream" because you have to be in a state of permanent sleep to believe it.

Don't believe it.

Do something about it. [scattered laughter; scattered applause]

Do something about it! [applause; scattered shouting]

Do something!

One day, you have to wake up and do something.

What I did was start collecting a dossier, a file I kept on my home screen.

Whenever I saw what Eddie Glass was describing 100 years or so ago happening today, in our up-to-the-nano world, I put it there. After a few months I had to stop. Without trying, just by keeping my eyes open to what came through my various feeds, I had collected more than 700 of these things! My arm memory was running low!

That's when I realized that Eddie Glass was for-realzies. But even he couldn't have imagined how far we've come along since his times. We've evolved. We've improved. Now our PWRS are better than ever!

Everyone else isn't. But that's not what matters. What matters is that everything is working the way it's supposed to work, just as my paternal grandparents on the Galt side fantasized it might.

And I have the evidence.

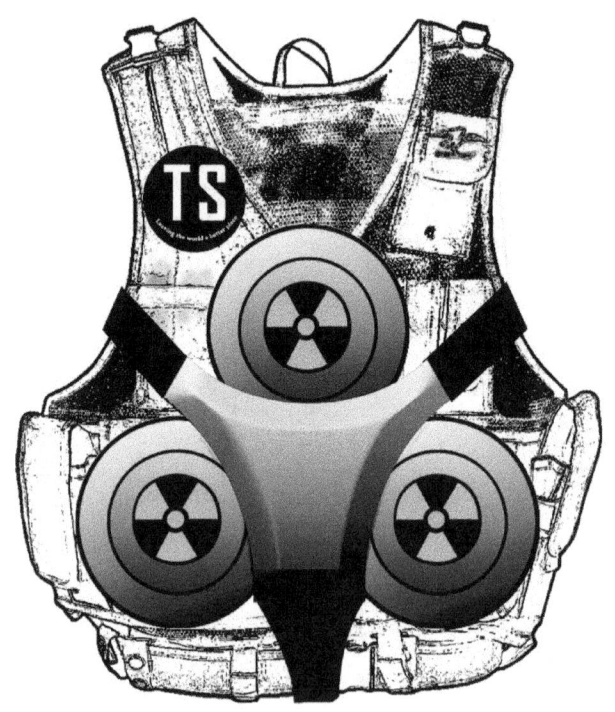

Evidence #1

You've probably seen my Uncle Jason on the news updates. He's considered a trusted source, an authoritative voice. Whenever the content providers have a story involving world finance, they call my Uncle Jason and he says reassuring and smart things. And somehow he usually manages to slip the words "under the stewardship of China Bank™" into his sound bites. He's a smoothie.

Uncle Jason looks like a Bartlett's pear stuffed into a bespoke suit one size too small. It doesn't matter that his body fat ratio is so far over the official threshold that he's disqualified from National Health coverage. He can afford his own medical staff, courtesy of China Bank™ and its benevolent compensation committee.

Jason Barclay is very well taken care of, even if he doesn't take care of himself.

So is my Uncle George, who looks pretty much like Jason does. Twins will be that way, I guess.

Both George and Jason have slaves that they call servants. They also have servants they call drivers and assistants. And they have many assistants to assist them in avoiding contact with the people who work for them. This constellation of "help" is in charge of making sure the only exertions the Barclay boys endure is piling more money onto their tower of success.

They also both have personal trainers who are paid handsomely to yell at them, like a dominatrix specializing in verbal humiliation.

I mentioned all the doctors…

They both own priceless Basquiats and Rod Smiths, which hang in their (tax-deductible) Barclay Galleries Moderne, which is open to the public periodically, and therefore is a civic contribution, not a personal warehouse.

Although they both live above Google™ Park in penthouse apartments with indoor swimming ponds, they're officially residents of Macao. How that works I'm not sure. I do know that living in Macao gracefully lowers their income tax rate from 44% to 6%.

This is helpful, because although Jason and George Barclay between them are worth about Y$11 billion, give or take a few hundred million, you can never have enough.

There are worthy charities to support, baubles to acquire, lives to impact. And even more important, there's measuring to be done. How much? How well? How well did they achieve and how much did they achieve? There's one acceptable way to measure that: add it up. Biggest number wins.

I would like to stress and emphasize: my uncles Jason and George Barclay are *not* criminals. Although they've ruined countless lives with famously ruthless foreclosures (supposedly ordered by the bosses in Beijing) and collected usurious amounts of interest, neither man has ever been convicted, let alone charged, with any sort of crime. They're model citizens, which I know because there's a wall at the Barclay Moderne dedicated to their honorary doctorates and "Man of the Year" citations.

They're very nice to my birth mother, their sister, Elaine. But if you ask them, "Who is Joan Galt?" they say something like, "I don't know, but that sounds like a good story!" or "This is not someone I'm familiar with personally."

To them, I'm the mistake that never happened. I'm the niece they didn't want.

Elaine tells me she doesn't approve of their attitude and, supposedly, she refused to talk with either one for several years as a kind of protest. Eventually, I guess, they patched things up. Jason sent her a giant red velvet cake with the word LANIE spelled out in sweet cream meringue; George sent her a (smallish) rhino-ivory backscratcher, and suddenly everything was all better.

But they still don't acknowledge my existence.

That used to trouble me.

No, worse than that. It used to piss me off. Just boiling rage, like I could hurt someone, or myself.

I came to understand, though, that my Uncles Jason and George couldn't help themselves. They were born to be Barclays. This is their programming. They're doing exactly what their DNA is instructing them to do.

We must have compassion for them. They're not villains.

They're victims.

Evidence #2

For one insane summer, while I was still at The Harvard™, I did an unpaid internship at The Robb Club®. That's not meant to be a humble brag.

Back in those naïve days, I was still interested in "hospitality" – the hotel business. I guess I envisioned myself being the stern-but-kind matriarch of a large "family" of employees. (Thank you, six years of therapy!) Also, I just like hotels.

Working at the Robb for a summer was considered a golden entry on your resume. *Everyone* wanted to work there (for free). You kept reminding yourself of this after it dawned on you after two days of electronic filing duty that your amazing career opportunity was actually going to be forty-hours-a-week of what amounted to slave labor, "managing" the whims of the members, who collectively controlled New York, and, thus, about half the world.

I wasn't allowed to talk to any of these noble gentlemen. I worked mostly in the back, "administrating," as they called it. But I came to know the members intimately through their Member Profile, which was kept on file so that we who served them might somehow serve them better.

These were the most valuable men in American society. These were the super winners worth thousands of average men combined. Yet, oddly, none of them wanted "the public" to know that they were an esteemed member of The Robb Club®. Perhaps they were afraid of anarchist paint-bombs being strewn on them. Or maybe they had earned (and literally paid for) more privacy rights than the rest of us. Right now, I don't care. I feel it's important for the world to know who some of the most valuable men on the planet are – and why they're so valuable!

The list, as I'm sure you can see, is scanned directly [and illegally; whatever] from The Robb Club®'s digital ledger. The annotations are mine.

Paul Imark: He made his billions as the founder of Labor Patrol™. There were already several companies specializing in prison labor. Mr. Imark was the one who added to the employment pool OSHA-certified Lazy Americans® who exhibited no signs of wishing to achieve.

Vikram Blanjiani: Do you remember when bus rape video was considered edgy? Those were the days before Mr. Blanjiani created and subsequently conquered the market for "surveillance content." Now that almost every corporation in America counts on the revenue stream from licensing of their surveillance footage, we get to watch countless rapes and murders occurring around the world, and Mr. Blanjiani gets to be richer.

Dale Smith: The visual counter on your shoulder that displays your individual likes and key stats? That was him.

Craig Lugello: Who doesn't know Cranky Craig? The (self-proclaimed) "King of Weight Loss" built an empire on insulting fat people. That one commercial, the screaming one? That's Mr. Lugello: "Are you serious? Do you really want to lose weight? Then, CONSUME FEWER CALORIES THAN YOU BURN! Eat less. Exercise more. Do it!"

Tanner Hutchings, III: Old money. Buildings.

Investment funds. Umbrella companies. What he actually did (or does) I cannot say. Another resident of Macao visiting New York.

Jamieson Johnson, Jr: Known around the club as "3J." Heir to a cosmetics and hygiene fortune from the 20th Century. Expert gin rummy player, accomplished lothario, single malt whisky connoisseur. Philanthropist. Cause supporter. Highly admired by fellow magnates for his ability to keep up appearances.

K. Addison Bailey: Palm oil.

Frankie Ascona, IV: Copper.

David Ainheist: He runs Black Hole Capital, the hedge fund. Much of their holdings are concentrated in drone companies, but they own parts of everything - so Mr. Ainheist owns parts of everything.

Bob Pooley: Pooley Properties, that's him. Biggest landlords in New York, New Delhi, and Shanghai. Mr. Pooley collects rental income from nearly 360,000 tenants. His litigiousness is legendary and much admired by the members of The Robb.

J'Donnie Hardaway: They made a movid about him, with Kumaki Reed doing the honors.[20] The story: His parents were famous progressive nature warrior folks, who were orthodoxly non-violent and vegan. He grew up on a commune in the Free Republic of California. Home-schooled. Pantheistic. Then, like most kids, when he was a little older, Mr. Hardaway rebelled. Hard. He bathed twice a day. He drove an antique fossil-fuel-burning SUV.[21] He took a job at a bank. He became President of

---

[20] Wasn't that great, I heard. Didn't download it.
[21] Sports Utilization Vehicle, a kind of truck they used to make when there was gasoline.

that bank, and very rich. That
bank figured out how to
"appropriate" the land that the
Hardaway homestead
occupied. Mr. Hardaway's
parents now work for him.

Bradley Zallmatt: The
"father of the personal missile."

Michael Blumberg: Heir to
some immense fortune (semi-
conductors?) looked after by
minions while he follows his
passions: wine, trout fishing,
and population culling -
mostly in Africa, with Mr.
Zallmat's premium line of
personal weaponry.

David Guy: Another heir
to another fortune built by
another generation.

These splendid achievers opened my eyes.
The Robb Club® membership included some of the
wealthiest men (no women!) in America.
Entrepreneurs. Titans. At the time, I understood
implicitly that their innate intelligence and genius
radiated outward, allowing those of us who came in

contact with their penumbra of excellence to become slightly more excellent ourselves. This all seemed obvious to me. I mean, these men had achieved more than thousands of other men *combined.* Indeed, this was why they were *worth more* than thousands of men combined. Their net worth, I mean.

But also the other way, too. Their WorthScore©. They were obviously of *greater value* to society than thousands of other men combined, because that's the way we do it: we've arranged ourselves to reward the more valuable among us with more of life's bounty. That's always been the fairest thing to do.[22]

So I listened closely that summer at The Robb. I paid attention. Kept my ears wide open.

Also, I kept my arm wide open – in capture mode. Is that a torturable offense?

Recording wasn't permitted inside the Club, of course. I knew I was being naughty. But, at the time, I was an innocent ingénue in search of wisdom, or, short of that, the secret to winning in the Game of Life.

I consider one conversation I overheard during a slow, multi-stop elevator ride from the club's penthouse down to 5th Avenue to be a defining moment in my worldview. *This is copied from an old algo-drive stored on the usual archive sites, in case the forensic minded want to verify.* Let me assure you, although the two gentlemen

---

[22] And probably always will be, unless someone has a better idea.

126

involved may have been slightly drunk on single malt, they were fully aware of my presence as they delivered their discourse. Almost like it was meant as a charitable donation toward my ongoing education.

2081-7-01; 18:02

Tanner Hutchings, III: Thank God for Islay! And hurrah for Havana!

David Guy: My pleasure...It takes the sting out of everyday rudeness, doesn't it?

Tanner Hutchings, III: I have no complaints – except, did we get on the wrong elevator? The, uh, local?[23]

David Guy: Oopsie Whisky wins again.

Tanner Hutchings, III: We can get off, take the local back *up*, and then catch the –

David Guy: It's fine. No complaints.

Tanner Hutchings, III: Me either. It just seems like everyone *else* does. You know? Always complaining instead of, you know, *doing*. I mean, I get it. The frustration. But, really, does the complaining accomplish anything?

David Guy: About the...?

---

[23] Programmed to stop frequently on the way down to collect workers. Not meant for Club members, who had their own "express" elevator.

Tanner Hutchings, III: Anything. The members of this club. Winners. Aren't we all doing important things?

David Guy: Maybe in some cases.

Tanner Hutchings, III: Which is why I don't understand the complaining. The sniveling.

David Guy: By the –

Tanner Hutchings, III: You know, the *whining*. The pitiful rhetorical questions.

David Guy: They say you can't teach common sense.

Tanner Hutchings, III: Precisely. So if I were to ask you...Is the banker's work more important than the work done by, I don't know, someone's *aunt*, the emergency room nurse? Or by your friend's *mom*, the elementary school teacher? By the farmer who grows your crickets? Isn't in some ways our work *more important* than all their work combined?

David Guy: *(chuckling, chortling)* The answer, I'm afraid, is yes. Yes, of course bankers, financiers -- we *are* more valuable than everyone you know, because we have the most money.

Tanner Hutchings, III: It seems self-evident.

David Guy: Numbers don't lie. They don't have opinions. They *are* opinions.

128

Numbers confirm society's opinion of who we are and what we're worth.

Tanner Hutchings, III: Isn't that the definition of being rich?

David Guy: That is.

Tanner Hutchings, III: The question is, Why isn't this explained properly to the younger generation? Why have our schools failed to deliver this message, you know, *widely*?

David Guy: It's a mystery.

Tanner Hutchings, III: My grandparents – and this made an impression on me. They, at a very young age, I must have been ten? They gave me some books to read on the power of individual human initiative. [24]

David Guy: Ah, yes.

Tanner Hutchings, III: It was all true, you know. These books. They helped me see the truth: We properly value each member of society by allowing the marketplace to decide who and what is worth more.

David Guy: That's our system, right?

Tanner Hutchings, III: Hole-diggers make the mandated minimum; supervisors of hole-diggers make more. And the people who own the company that employees the

---

[24] They seemed to have the same taste in literature as *my* grandparents, the Galts.

supervisors of the hole-diggers make even more.

David Guy: It may not be pretty, but it works. You punish people for not being smart enough to own companies and reward others for being smart enough to avoid manual labor.

Tanner Hutchings, III: I'll tell you what's wrong with America –

David Guy: Too much regulation.

Tanner Hutchings, III: Yes, that, of course. But – and I'm sure you remember this. Americans used to *work*. They put in a solid eight hours, and usually more.

David Guy: At a fair price.

Tanner Hutchings, III: A decent price.

David Guy: Now *everyone* wants to be a landlord!

Tanner Hutchings, III: I'll tell you what the problem is. Everyone wants to be a landlord and no one wants to work.

David Guy: Laziness.

Tanner Hutchings, III: That's what it is. People don't seem to understand that you can't get someone else to work for you, to do all the work, until you've worked yourself into that position.

David Guy: How can someone work for you if you can't pay him?

Tanner Hutchings, III: Exactly. My message would be: you've got to work hard

before you can get others to work for you,
unless you're exclusively going after brown
foreigners. Those are always cheaper.

David Guy: Portugal.

Tanner Hutchings, III: Right.

David Guy: Not everyone can be a
landlord.

Tanner Hutchings, III: No. But we can
all try.

David Guy: That's the beauty of it. The
poetry.

Tanner Hutchings, III: D-Guy, my
friend, some achieve, some do not.

David Guy: Not everyone can be a
landlord...Hup! Here we are...[*leering at me*]
After you young lady...OK, Tanzer. See you in
Macao? We should think about
[unintelligible]...

Tanzer and D-Guy. They're right, you
know. Not everyone can own the world. That's just
not mathematically possible if you want there to be
an adequate number of billionaires on the planet.

So if what you're after is to get through life
being properly valued by everyone else, it sure
helps if you've got the right genes.

Evidence #3

We all know Warren Singh is famously modest and unassuming. He attributes that to his mother, Jennifer Singh (formerly Hansen), who taught him not to be showy. How nice that he doesn't flaunt his unfathomable wealth and power. He just goes about his business, which is to collect more wealth and power.

Warren Singh is just a regular guy who happens to own everything.

His son Rajiv "Roger" Singh and his daughter Shiva Singh-Schlimovitz are aggressively, passionately *not* regular.

Remember when Roger bought two nuclear-powered aircraft carriers?[25] That was fabulous and outrageous and fabulously outrageous, but what was

---

[25] His and hers. One for him, one for his plaything at the time, former Ms. Universe Conchita Jones. Pretty sure he took the ship back when they broke up, right?

going to stop him? We (the government, the national treasury) needed cash after the near-collapse of the prison industry. Same deal with Jamaica, when they were bought by his younger sister Shiva. They needed the money; she needed something new to own. It all worked out.

Apparently the siblings are very close. They live in the same building in New York, near the old detention center on Governor's Island, across from the remains of the Statue of Liberty. I'm sure you've seen the pictures. Their quaint Bro-Sis crash-pad in Manhattan is, like 45 stories tall. (Just looked it up: it's actually 44, which is supposed to be lucky). All this living space is useful, because they have to share it with Shiva's children from her first failed marriage.

It has two helipads, six high-speed elevators, a personal bungee jump, and nearly 2,000,000-square-feet of video billboard space. The outdoors advertising income alone is worth millions a year. Roger and Shiva don't need the money, of course. But, still, it's not like they're going to turn it down – or donate the outside of their building to a community solar bank. The whole point of being a Singh is to add another stack of money to the stacks you already have piled in your skyscraper.

Another reason they need to acquire more wealth – which, NewSource© estimated flows to them at the rate of about Y$117,000 per hour, round-the-clock – is that the area just around and beside their beautiful home isn't so nice. Very messy. Squalid, you might say if you were impolite.

Smelly, actually.

The problem is there's a homeless encampment of nearly 10,000 bums and losers at the foot of Roger and Shiva's gleaming tower.

What an eyesore it must be to look out of your floor-to-ceiling windows and have to encounter such filth, all those constant reminders of how terribly unsuccessful people can turn out when they don't really try hard enough.

What's a multi-billionaire's son or daughter to do? Well, some impertinent progressive types made the galling suggestion that the Singhs could improve their view *and* their sense of regal patronage if they would build several modest housing units in the blocks around their tower. It would have cost about Y$68 million to provide cell shelter for all 10,000 street squatters, as well as an appropriately sized *solarsource* to power the thing.

Roger and Shiva assured everyone that this wasn't about the money. It was about the principle. And so they unleashed their lawyers and lobbyists to get something done. Last report I saw, the kids had spent nearly Y$114 million in legal fees and the homeless encampment was still there. Now it's like 12,000 unwashed souls.

On the face of it, you might conclude that the Singhs have overspent. But can you really overspend when you're fighting for your rights? *The hundreds of millions that could have been used to build shelters went to lawyers.*

When you think about it, that's the way things are *supposed* to work. The most valuable people got the money, not the interchangeable ones on the bottom, the ones who we don't value and who don't deserve it.

Uncle Warren Singh was reportedly mortified at all the fuss. This was not the way he would have handled things. Not like this. So publicly. He would have made the problem go away quietly.

But Rajiv and Shiva Singh couldn't help themselves. They were just doing what their genes were telling them to do. The genes they got from our dear old Uncle Warren.

Premonition Vision 3

"Place the ring around your Termite switch," Dylan tells me. I reach down and find it beneath my dress. The ring slips right over it, just like a condom is supposed to when you've got it right-side-up. I can feel the ring snap into place, flush against the interior fabric of my Endvest™.

"A final safety precaution," Dylan explains. "You've been authenticated, secured, and engaged. Nothing bad can happen now. No accidents. Only the plan."

"Oh, that's marvelous," I reply, because it really is marvelous how everything eventually works out for the best, as though there's a Master Plan and there's someone smart and able enough to execute it.

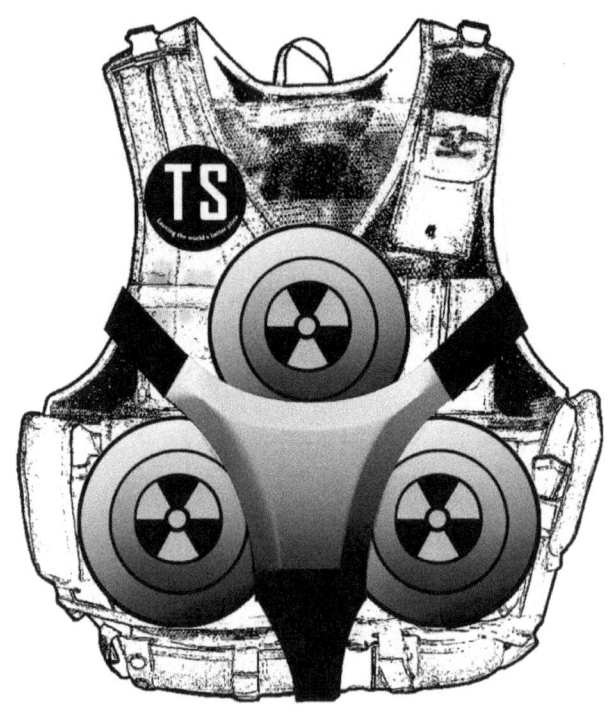

Hoarders

When I got hooked on watching banned Truthteller Rants, I also became fascinated in general with popular art and culture around the turn of the century. Let me tell you, that was a *strange* moment in time.

Here's a strange fact: way back in the Age of Television, there was a popular form of programming known as "freak shows." These were mostly about people born with congenital defects, like conjoined twins, or about mentally ill people and their entertaining habits, because, let's face it, the mentally ill can be pretty amusing.

According to the Wiki, one of America's favorites was a program called "//Happy Hoarding." It was about seemingly normal human beings who, unfortunately, had some sort of short-circuit in the their brain that compelled them to continually acquire more stuff, even after they had no more room to store all their stuff.

There were episodes about a man whose trailer home was stacked floor-to-ceiling with newspapers, one for each day of his life.[26] He had little tunnels he could crawl through to get from the paper-filled kitchen to the paper-filled living room. Another one was about a lady who collected cats – real ones. She lived in a 300-square-foot studio apartment, but she couldn't stop herself from adopting more cats, even after she already had 129 of them. Other episodes were about hoarders without a fetish, indiscriminate hoarders, human black holes, people who wanted *everything* within their grasp, no matter how valueless or useless. To these sickos, *all* things were valuable. Cats, newspapers, empty plastic bottles – whatever. They wanted it all. "Happy Hoarding" was about how the crazy find a form of happiness by clinging to material possessions.

Here's another strange and related fact: Despite the regularity of natural disasters in the area, what remains of the California coastline is still considered the most prized real estate in the world. Oceanfront property. Beaches. Exclusive. Magic. Although almost nobody can afford it, many, many people would like to have a home on the coast, now that we're close to figuring out the whole earthquake thing. Even more people would like access to the few miles of beaches that remain around Los Angeles and Ventura, or to one of the lagoons of downtown San Diego. Millions of local residents – you might call them "the public" –

---

[26] Newspapers, as in "real paper." This was before Armscreens.®

would like to visit a place they used to call "public beaches."

Unfortunately, that's not possible. These days the beachfront lots are private property, with a funny story to go along with them.

Rajiv Singh, the celebrated son, brother, and "conscientious billionaire" of the esteemed Singh family, has been quietly acquiring these lots for the past 12 years. "Microchip Beach," they call it, in honor of the tiny device that allowed the landlords of the coast to become fabulously wealthy enough to become the landlords of the coast. There's only, like, 40 of the lots between what used to be Santa Monica and the metropolis of Ventura. And of these only like 30 of them have direct access to sand and unpolluted water. Clever Roger has bought 26 of them, investing nearly Y$800 million in the process! Some of these lots don't even have mansions on them; they're just "wild" two-acre rectangles on promontories overlooking the new Pacific sea wall. And they're all his.

A group of my impolite hacker friends (*not* Jonah), were able to get past the firewall on the public ownership records, which were locked and sequestered on politeness grounds.[27]They discovered that behind the shell companies listed on the official paperwork was one naughty yet lovable

---

[27] It's wonderful to have lived in a day and age when deference to hurt feelings allows rich people to have their dealings shielded from inquiring eyes. And even more wonderful that the bribes they pay in the form of "community support" goes to sweetening the National Lottery™.

playboy-entrepreneur-philanthropist. They posted their findings on //Assange4evah.com. They issued a manifesto that declared unequivocally that Greed is a terrible thing. "Greed is why we still use Portuguese slaves. Greed is why we turn debtor nations into stitching colonies," they wrote. "Greed is why we educate the masses just well enough that they behave, but not well enough that they might all transform themselves into high achievers."

Roger initially had no official comment, although an open microphone at a public board meeting caught him explaining to a sympathetic fellow billionaire that, "We can't *all* be rich, you know! Without a permanent lower caste, who will serve?"

As sensible as this line of thinking seems, Roger's media managers quickly changed his mind, getting him to see that, actually, everyone could be rich, in a manner of speaking. With the help of his professional message shapers, he graciously explained his actions: [*verbatim, copy-and-pasted from his feed*] "I'm acquiring the Los Angeles coastline to ensure that generations of children and their hot and sweaty parents have access to the ocean, as well as the fabulous beaches beside it that will be intermittently accessible."

So, to everyone's relief, what looked on the surface to be a modern episode of "Happy Hoarding" was actually another generous and civic-minded public betterment project.

The alternative is less cheerful, isn't it? It's sort of upsetting to think how sick someone must be to keep 129 cats in a studio apartment.

There were rumors that the public beaches would open in January of 2089, last year. That there would be weekend-long celebrations, and dancing, and laser shows. There were rumors that one particularly prized stretch of beach – nearly a half-mile long – just down the hill from the 405-podway, would be dedicated to children and named "Roger's Resort" in honor of the great and generous Roger Singh, who, the rumors suggested, was embarrassed by all the fuss. He was just "doing the right thing," just like his daddy Warren would.

When the official media outlets sought comment, Mr. Singh's spokesman issued another modest "no comment," and asked that the family's privacy be respected during "a difficult decision-making time."

That was 17 months ago, when many, many people still had the utmost confidence that Roger Singh, not being mentally ill or anything, was working feverishly to make the dream of public beaches a reality. He was confronting environmental regulations and other time-wasting complications, not to mention the logistics involved in building new transportation hubs. And herding lawyers. It was complicated.

Which is why it was somehow decided that the whole project would work better, more efficiently, if and when Roger owned *all 40* of the available oceanfront parcels. It would be less complicated that way. Fewer cooks making the soup. Fewer agendas. Indeed, only one agenda: getting the real estate properly developed, so generations of families could once again enjoy the

143

splendors of California's unique topographic wonders, the confluence of land and sea.

That, of course, could take some time. Not every property owner on Microchip Beach is as cooperative as the prospective new owner wishes they would be. One loony old crone, a "settler" back in 2052, after San Andreas 2, said she would never sell to Rajiv Singh, his associates, or – and this you can look up – "anyone else who belongs to their elite club."

Discussions continue.

Just last month I got an alert. From Roger's official feed: [*verbatim, copy and pasted*] "**The project that others are calling 'Roger's Resort' is going to be a reality! Happy to announce that we've made arrangements so that when I die the property will be transferred into a blind trust dedicated to building playgrounds for disadvantaged inner-city children. Each playground will have a public swimming pool, so kids can have a beach experience without harming the fragile ecosystem around the coastline. This is a big win for everyone! #4thekids**"

It's so great how everything works out for the best, isn't it?

This is what I keep telling myself, what I've been telling myself every night when I stare at the ceiling and review my plan. I envision my entrance, I see my encounter, and then… the final moment. And I keep telling myself, *everything will be for the best*.

You could say this is a big win for everyone.

Sudden Sadness

I'm sorry if this has gone on too long. I really just wanted to set the record totally straight before I no longer can. I want everyone to understand why this had to happen.

So, again, my apologies for the rambles. I ask your patience for a girl who won't ask anything of you ever again. *Namaste.*

I was just now looking at a picture of me and Jonah, smiling and laughing. We look so young. So happy. You can tell that we're in love.

Now, I'm really sad.

I have no other choice. The choice has been made. There's no going back now.

But I'm really, really sad.

You can understand that, right?

This is a beautiful world. In *so* many ways. And I'm going to miss it. Oh, how I'm going to miss it when I'm gone.

I'm determined and I'm certain. But still.

You know this is the hardest thing I'll ever do.

The Marcy Connection

Actual TexThought® conversation between me and Marcy Kim. Copy and pasted. Slightly embarrassing, but important enough for the historical record that I can deal with it.

Joan: Thinking about you.

Marcy: Last time you told me that you wanted "boundaries" in our relationship. So?

Joan: I can think about my friends! I do consider you a friend.

Marcy: OK. Me, too. Ur like sister.

Joan: Yes. The yoga, food, music, hiking and holistic medicine are things we both enjoy. And Jonah, of course.

Marcy: LOL.

Joan: ☺ And, btw, he's totally not freaked out or anything.

Marcy: Abt?

Joan: Marcy, in my spiritual quest, I've been striving to become a more & more good & kind human being, and one of its tenets, I believe, is honesty, and so I wanted to share this with you...I'm really sorry if having a genuine and sincere friendship is mistaken for something else. I do consider you, Marcy, a friend.

Marcy: Likewise.

Joan: The fact that you closely resemble one of my ex-girlfriends (I'm bi) isn't any sort of big deal in my mind.

Marcy. OK. Good.

Joan: A little distracting. ☺

Marcy: LOL.

Joan: Whatchya doin?

Marcy: Work.

Joan: At home?

Marcy: No. Still here.

Joan: OMG

Marcy: Yes. Looking into something. Might have found something.

Joan: ???

Marcy: A gene. Possibly.

Joan: ??? For?

Marcy: So, what are *you* doing tonight?

Joan: Nothing.

Marcy: Nothing? That doesn't sound like you.

Joan: I mean, nothing, you know...

Marcy: Do you want to keep me company?

Joan: Now?

Marcy: Yes. Maybe you would find this interesting?

Joan: I find you very interesting and the work you do is very interesting to me. You know that! I think that's why we're building a lifelong friendship. I really feel like we're on the same wavelength.

Marcy: So are you coming?

Joan: Are you sure you wouldn't be distracted if I was there?

Marcy: Only in a good way.

Joan: ☺

Marcy: ☺ Just buzz me when you arrive so I can get you in.

Joan: OK

Marcy: OK. Going back to work. You take care. Get here safe.

Joan: OK.

Being real: I wasn't really focused at the time on what was happening in Marcy's lab. I was more focused on the person in Marcy's lab. I just found Marcy Kim extremely interesting. Fascinating is maybe not too strong of a word.

I didn't tell Jonah where I was going. Actually, I lied to him.[28] I made up some dumb thing involving Megan, a planning meeting for a protest. "She needs my input and energy."

I'm not sure why I did this. Jonah was always very encouraging of my relationship with Marcy. He introduced us! I guess sometimes I just want potentially complicated situations to be simple. Path of least resistance.

I don't know. All I can say is I hope you take my candidness about fibbing to Jonah, lying to him about seeing a girl I was attracted to, as a sign not of my momentary dishonesty but of my overall trustworthiness. Please don't think that my admission about lying to the love of my life makes me an unreliable reporter. THIS IS ALL TRUE. Everything I have written. Please remember that when they try to discredit me.

What did I expect was going to happen when I visited Marcy? I'm not really sure. But, yes, I was excited. The not knowing was the best part.

When I got there, after swiping in and getting scanned, most of the lab was quiet. The main hallway was dim, except for the light emanating from Marcy's area, the door cracked open, a shaft of whiteness slicing out. I knocked, and the door swung open gently.

"Hello, Joan," she said, smiling nervously.

---

[28] I feel icky about this. So sorry, dearest Jonah.

"Hello, Marcy," I said, searching her eyes for a signal.

"Good to have a friend here."

I took this as a sign that she wanted me to hug her, in a friendly way. "Good to be here," I said, embracing her. She smelled like lemons and salt.

"I've been working," she said. "Pretty intense."

"Poor baby."

She chuckled. "No, it's OK. I'm OK."

"Do you need a neck massage?"

"Stop it. Do you want to see this – it's…" she gestured toward a large screen near her desk, and stepped toward it, motioning for me to follow. Marcy inhaled. "So these are, like, visualizations of gene sequences. They're representations, right? It's, like, a graphics approach to looking at very small bits of information."

I nodded. She was so passionate about her work. I found that inspiring.

"So you can see, naked eye, all collated. Very useful." Marcy pointed to two rows of blocks and tubes. "Almost completely identical. But, here, in this region." She circled one section with her finger. "Right here you can see it. Can you see it?"

I leaned in. Lemons and salt again. "What am I looking for?"

"That little parallelogram thingie? How it's on the left one but not the other one?" Our faces were close. I felt I could detect the heat of her cheek near mine. We both looked straight ahead.

I peered in closely. Marcy's map was like a lung x-ray, but with far more vivid detail. The thingie wasn't hard to spot. "Oh, yes. Right there. Sure."

She leaned in. "So, yeah. That's sort of what I'm exploring at the moment." She looked at me then.

I don't know who kissed who first. It just happened. The way it does when it's just so right that it can't be wrong.

It was one long delicious soft kiss. That's all. Then we stopped.

Don't apologize for what just happened, I thought. Marcy looked at me, and I told her with my eyes, "Don't apologize."

She seemed to nod slightly, perceptibly. "Yeah." She said, nodding more.

I nodded, too.

We looked at each other for a second. I felt like I wanted to lean in and kiss her again, harder this time.

"So, anyway, yeah, this is what I'm working on," Marcy said, as though she had never been interrupted.

"It's very interesting," I said. "What you're working on."

"It is."

I chuckled. "What is it?"

"A gene sequence. A chunk from the genome. Recently discovered by a hobbyist in North Dakota. Recently, like, in the last year." She nodded.

"What does it represent?" I asked.

"Oh, I can't tell you that part!" she said, scowling at me in mock disapproval, as though she was shocked that I would even ask.

"Marcy, come on. It's not like I'm going to tell anyone. We all work for the same team. Hello!"

She shook her head. "*Joan.*"

"A cancer gene? Predisposes you to…"

Marcy smiled. "No, no. That's old stuff, girl. We got *that*."

"Yeah, I know. Cancer causes jobs."

"Right."

"So this new one, the mutant gene – it's a disease time bomb?"

Marcy went silent. "I guess you could say that."

I started to wonder why we – America, the CIA – were working on this DNA stuff. What were we going to do with it? What was the practical purpose?

Asking Marcy was useless. I knew she wouldn't tell me. At least not until I brought her to a state of complete surrender.

I don't know why certain women make me want to dominate them. They just trigger something. I took in all of Marcy Kim with my eyes and my nose. I wanted more. "What are you doing?" I asked her, grinning.

"I told you. It's –"

"No. I mean right now. Like, after you're done showing me your gene project?"

"Oh. Well, I was probably going to, I don't know, probably just go home?"

I looked her in the eye. I saw the whole picture, the way it would unspool. I knew I could make it happen. I knew I was permitted to be bold. "That's great," I said. "We're going. I'm taking you home."

Shiva Singh-Schlimovitz Knows Best

We talked about the brother, Rajiv. Now, his older sister, our national role model. Go to her official site. Right there on the Home Page: "I may not know how to pick husbands, but I know what's best for our country!"

I think she's being funny? #irony

Facts: The marriages. She's had three of them, so far. None of these husbands has lasted longer than two years. Kept first-husband's name for the children (two boys, Babatunde and Irving, now 12 & 13). Left the other two fellows ruined (financially) thanks to unimpeachable pre-nuptial agreements. Famously outspoken. Opinionated. Confident ("I have sixty-billion reasons to believe in my problem-solving ability," also on her Website). The richest woman in North America – and just behind Gong-Lin Fung over-all.

Shiva Singh-Schlimovitz has a gravity about her, you might say.

She's someone we should listen to. And that's not just me saying it, that's Shiva. "I can help," she always promises, "if you would only *listen.*"

You can understand how frustrating it must be for her, knowing what needs to be done, owning all sorts of evidence that she knows better than the average girl about how the game is played. Yet the people who haven't succeeded at any measurable level, the people who really need the help, her guidance – well, they *just don't listen.* You can understand how this is all rather bothersome.

Have you reviewed the Practical Advice page at her site? My favorite: "If you're jealous of those with more money than you, don't just sit there and complain. Do something! Do something to make money. Make more for yourself. Spend less time drinking, or smoking, or whatever it is you do. Socializing. Just achieve more."

Her position on the proposed "super tax" on annual dividend income over Y$12 million: "Axe the tax!"

Is she an heiress? "My father gave me and my brother a small stake to get started. Thanks to hard work, good moral character, and, yes, a little bit of luck, I've managed to grow my father's investment several hundred times over."

Her greatest accomplishment (aside from her babies)? "Creating jobs. Thousands of them." This really is quite a great feat, because every job Shiva Singh-Schlimovitz conjures from the ether not only makes her incrementally richer, thanks to her perch at the top of the labor pyramid, it also means one less miserable human being sleeping on public streets.

She pays well, too. Usually more than the mandated minimum wage, sometimes as much as 14% above the minimum. She doesn't have to do this. To Shiva, it's just a small way to give back to the community. That and the museums she's fond of constructing, purpose-built to warehouse (and display) her expanding holdings.[29]

Some noisemakers have complained that Shiva's acquisitiveness shouldn't necessarily be subsidized by public taxes. But that kind of jibber-jabber usually becomes a whisper and a memory. One of the sixty-billion reasons to avoid disagreeing with Shiva Singh-Schlimovitz is that she views lawyers as nicely dressed toys, interchangeable soldiers that are fun to play with, especially when they're suing people Shiva dislikes.

Under different circumstances, I would be seriously afraid to write all this about Shiva. Bankrupting enemies is one of her favorite hobbies. Defamation being a serious offense.

I'm doomed, so whatever.

Unfortunately, *so are you*. Everyone is.

---

[29] In addition to art and gems and original documents (two Guttenberg Bibles, a "rough draft" of the U.S. Constitution), SSS has the biggest collection of live, functional kidneys in the world, which she generously displays to the public six-days-a-week, eight-hours-a-day, with no admission charged.

But not from climate change, or Canadian hegemony. "America is doomed," Shiva reminds us. "America is doomed if we do not lower taxes, cut regulations, limit mandated wages, and encourage investment in businesses run by people who know how to run a business. Inequality is what creates achievement. Nations depend on their health – economically, culturally and psychologically – upon the achievement of a comparatively small number of talented and determined people. We must let these people achieve!"

Many smart and forceful people agree with Shiva. Most of them work at a think tank or political action group endowed by her family foundation. Not that it matters. They're scientists and academics. We can trust them.

And you can trust me when I tell you that the simple solution to all the world's problems – poverty, disease, violence, all the big ones – is to correctly answer one vexing question: more or fewer?

Do we need more or fewer Shiva Singh-Schlimovitzs?

Jonah on the Record

Marcy = intense experience. Jonah = THE ONE.

Can I share the sweetest thing with you? One of the reasons I fell in love with Jonah was the letters he wrote me. And by "wrote me," I mean actually *writing* them, like typing and everything. #So20thCentury

I'm scanning in one of my favorites. So now it's part of the record. Government investigators will see it one way, and some of you, no doubt, will look at it as a kind of evidence, proof of Jonah's culpability or innocence. Others will see what true love looks like on a page.

What I see is a terrible paradox: How can any woman want to leave behind a man so utterly beautiful?

Crying now…

[I love you, Jonah. So sorry if this hurts you in any way. You know they're going to comb through all your feeds and make up something. You know how they do that. But they can't make up letters like this.]

May, 2090

My Dearest Jo-Jo,

I was thinking today: how did I ever get so lucky? How could one guy ever get so undeservedly lucky? What have I possibly done to earn a woman as spectacular and inspiring and, yes, scrumptious as you? I must have been Bill Birble in another life.

So I was in this tele-con with Dmitri and Ferdy (from the Hacktivista Collective), dealing with some issues – the usual. They were asking me my opinion of the most effective worm to deal with the China Bank [*ha! yes! it's true! got the wormblocker code from Darkstar; will try to share, but probably has built-in expiration*]. And do you know what I said? "I'm sorry," I said, "I know I should have been listening more carefully, but, dudes, sorry, stone cold truth: I was thinking about kissing Joanie's luscious lips."

Lotsa laughs. Ferdy: "All this time I was thinking how luscious *your* lips are, Jonah."

Dmitri: "Yeah, you're both pretty hot. But I like her long hair. Grow yours out, dude, you might look as good as her."

Me: "Not possible, bro. She's too fine!" Everyone agreed.

Anyway, just a little note to let you know that you're always on my mind, even when I'm supposed to be thinking about how to restore economic justice to the global economy.

Love you, Joanie. Proud of you.

Proud of *us*. It's pretty cool, isn't it? How two adopted kids found their way in this world, found their way to each other? I really think that having certain similarities — the dead father thing, of course — has let me understand you better than people who came from a more traditional background could. Know what I mean? I understand those abandonment fears...we all go through them, all of us. But I get it. I know how real it can feel. You're doing great.

The Termite Squad:
My Official and Authentic Report

YOU ARE A CHAMPION. The work you're doing with Woman Project, the solar sharing, and that's on top of whatever good works you're doing at your day job at the Think Tank ☺.

Plus, you're delicious.

I love you, Joan Galt. I'm glad you're mine to share with the world. You're going to be one of the greats. People will be talking about you for many years to come. And I feel honored that I was there at the start of your journey.

Love, love, love,

Your Man (and friend, and playmate and lover),

Jonah

He didn't know. He doesn't know. *He's innocent in every way.* Please, world, please show him mercy. Jonah is innocent.

Home Diagnosis

Despite what the official Wiki says, the cheap disposable over-the-counter DNA testers you can buy online are *not* as accurate as the ones you ship back to the lab with a drop of blood. They *are* more effective than the so-called "blow-and-go", the breathalyzer version, which, BTW, is really just analyzing saliva molecules, so you're better off just doing a cheek scrape.

Yes, I know a lot about DNA testers!

Most of what I know, I learned from Marcy. I took an interest in her work and she inadvertently educated me. And now I'm sharing. #goodkarma

That's actually how I'm looking at this whole thing: an act of sharing. I'm sharing my history and thoughts and explanations, so you won't have to wonder and try to fill in the blanks. Also, my Termite Squad service is a kind of sharing. It's definitely an act of giving.

And, no, I'm not getting all "fallen hero" on you. I'm just saying there's an element of sacrifice involved.

Even Jesus Christ recognized that there were sacrifices involved in his becoming humanity's savior. [Hard to tell in textype, but, no, I'm *not* being facetious. I'm serious.] JC was cool with how everything ended up, but he still took numerous opportunities to point out that he hoped his death wouldn't be in vain, that he knew he was giving up one thing to help bring about another. Am I making sense?

Anyway, I'm glad to share. Being of service. Doing something, not nothing.

Blood tests: the best way to get your genes mapped. Computer-analyzed lab blood tests: superior to do-it-yourselfers.

Why you need to know this. I'm going to tell you.

So, it's the night I've sort of been dreading, the one I knew had to arrive eventually but which I hoped I could forestall with positive thinking. It's the night that Marcy and Jonah and Joan are all going to be together. Not tele-con. Face2face. For *dinner*. #awkward!

It was Jonah's idea. After what happened with Marcy, I knew I had to tell him, and she knew she had to tell him, and we both knew that it had to be done, but neither of us had the courage, so somehow Jonah did it for us, as if he knew all along that we girls were destined to make a connection. He was the one who got it out in the open, out of the shadows. Just hearing him talk about it out loud

164

somehow made the subject less dangerous. Jonah's generosity of spirit made us three as comfortable as possible with the intense triangulation.

Plus, the thought of me and Marcy together he found incredibly hot. He's just an unashamed perv that way.

The main point, though, is that Jonah was OK with the hook-up, happy for the connection. And he thought we all should stay friends, and that all our relationships would be richer with Marcy staying in everyone's life.

Which all sounded chill in theory. But, you know, the physical presence/proximity issue. Like, it's hard to turn on and off (at least for me). It's not your arm. *That* I turned off before Marcy arrived at our place.

Jonah was pretty sure Marcy was still a vegan, but I insisted we put out cricket snacks anyway, just in case. It really, truly didn't bother me that my sweetheart knew Marcy better than I did. I was conflicted and weirded-out by certain stuff, but I was genuinely glad that she could stay in my life. Our lives.

I remember dusting off the *accumulation* (and the rest of our small art collection), straightening the clutter, and setting the table – fair-trade cloth napkins and everything – and all the time thinking that the best result in the world would be never having to choose between them.

Dinner went well. A little tense here and there. But overall a big relief. We *all* felt relieved, I think. All night I was super conscious of not looking too much at Marcy, avoiding eye contact, but also not being too obvious in my avoidance. No drama, no big moments. All very nice.

After dinner, which included two bottles of special occasion Virginia pure water for the three of us, the majority to Jonah, we were getting the vaporizer set up when Jonah asked Marcy if she ever did any tests on herself.

"Have I looked at my blood? Sure. Hasn't everyone?"

"Well, home-testing, yes," Jonah agreed. "But you know how that works. They only tell you so much. Breast cancer, baldness, your relationship to Thomas Jefferson. Not like a complete lab analysis."

Marcy said, "Right, I see what you're saying." It was a strange sort of mild turn-on to see them conversing together. As though they were colleagues, fellow experts – when secretly they were much more.

I just watched and listened. Enjoying, in a sick way.

Marcy stretched her neck from side-to-side, as though she were warming up for yoga. "With the understanding that I'm only permitted to discuss matters that don't pertain to my, you know, my work – you know, I have to…"

"Be discreet," Jonah said.

"Right." Marcy nodded. She glanced at me. I told her silently, *"Go ahead, girl. You can do it. Go ahead."*

She laughed nervously. "Well, discreetly, I've had the, uh, the opportunity to run a number of diagnostic tests on myself."

No one said anything.

Marcy looked at me. I raised an eyebrow, like, "*and…*"

"And," Marcy continued, "the results were in some ways quite amusing."

"Amazing?" Jonah asked.

"That, too… No, I said they were *amusing*, some of the results. You know, some unexpected things. Surprising things. Nothing major. So, yes, they were amusing. But also, OK, they were also *amazing* in that I felt, I feel like *I know myself better* now. Does that make sense?"

I nodded knowingly. Like, *if anyone understands, it's me.*

"Yes. Sure. What were some of the surprises?" asked Jonah.

"Yes! Tell us," I finally interjected.

Marcy giggled uncomfortably, shrugging. "I don't know. Like, for example – well, have you heard of an ancient Portuguese explorer – this is back when Portugal was actually a world power, no joke. His name was Ferdinand Magellan."

"Very familiar," Jonah said. "Me, too," I said. "Vaguely." #knowledgeispower

Marcy nodded again. "He stopped in Asia. Magellan did. And it turns out that I have what those of us in the splicing world call 'the Magellan gene.' It's actually identified by a numeric code that describes its sequencing. But, anyway, it's like a marker. If you have it, you're a direct descendant of Ferdinand Magellan, the Portuguese Conqueror. Which sounds funny in a modern context, I know. Anyway, I have it."

"So you've got the DNA of an imperialist-colonialist-crusader?" Jonah teased.

"Exactly! And I'm an explorer!"

I got a little twinge. They were so cute together. It made me sad and mad and glad simultaneously. I could feel their energy. It sort of knocked the wind out of me.

"Explorer. That's cool," Jonah said. "What else? Anything else, Miss Magellan?"

"Well, actually, I carry the Alzheimer's gene. So I know I'll need to start cannabis therapy pretty soon."

"Immediately!" Jonah said. We all laughed. Good times for sure.

Marcy said, "No, but I mean it's *good to know*. You know? It's good to have some advance warning for preventable things."

We agreed. "No doubt."

"And, also, from a less utilitarian perspective, it's like I was saying. I feel as though I know myself better. I know more about where I came from. Where I'm headed. Like, *who am I*? It's sort of right there in the code." Marcy shrugged. "A lot of it, anyway."

I could tell she loved being a DJ.

"I get it," Jonah said, grinning. "That's cool."

"Hey," I exclaimed, as though I were slightly drunk, which maybe I was, "Hey!" I said, "We should all get tested and see if we're all Magellans!"

"I'm definitely a Columbus," Jonah volunteered.

I shushed him. "No, seriously! We should do it. Can we do it? Marcy?"

She looked at Jonah, whose face totally said, "sure, of course, why not?"

Marcy grinned. "Sure," she said, looking in my eyes. "Of course, why not?"

"Seriously?" asked Jonah.

"He doesn't like giving blood samples," I explained. Not that anyone does. But in this age of sexually transmitted diseases, you get used to it if you want to stay safe. I've had the Sampler® feature activated on my arm since it came out, when I was still a teenager and thought I'd live forever. I think Daddy Peter even encouraged me to do my own blood testing, "just in case."

I pointed up the Sampler® on my arm. "I gotcha," I announced to Jonah, who seemed wary, slightly puzzled. He's not a recreational tester.

Placing my fingertip on the target spot, I felt the familiar intense heat, and it was done. "Voila," I said, displaying my fingertip, with one perfect pinhead of blood resting on it.

169

Marcy tilted her head sideways and said, "I'll get you a clean glass."

"Thanks, Mar," I said. "Here, Jonah. Just use my Sampler®."

"It's not that I don't like giving blood," Jonah stressed, giving me a limp finger, which I placed on the target. "It's just not my favorite – *yeeks*."

"Done," I said.

"Not my favorite thing." He held up his finger, with a little plummy pearl on top. We waved at each other, finger to finger, always pointing up.

Marcy returned with a glass in each hand. "Here you go," she said. "Just wipe your finger on the side. It's more than enough for me to work with."

We did, leaving scarlet streaks. Jonah's was a declining line. Mine was more squiggly.

Marcy capped the glasses and produced labels via TexThought® that said "Joan Galt, September, 90" and "Jonah Jones, September, 90." She applied them assuredly, as though she had handled these type of stickers many times before. That turned me on. Don't know why.

"That was easy," Marcy announced.

"So when?" I wondered aloud.

"Whenever. I mean, I could do it Monday morning and have the analysis ready Monday night. It's not that difficult."

Jonah nodded. "That's perfect. That's fast. Nice."

We all agreed the plan was copasetic. We made a tele-date for Monday night, 21:00. Three days later.

Marcy promised, "I'll have your results all categorized. And, yes, my dear Joan, we'll see if anyone else in this crowd is a descendant of a great conquering hero."

I said the first thing that came to my head. At the time, it probably sounded how it was supposed to: just one of those inane things we all say in the course of conversation. But now, in retrospect, I believe I must've had some sort of premonition or something. An advance understanding.

Because when Marcy said I'd get my results in three days, I said, like it was a dark joke, "Now I finally have something to look forward to in my life."

The Blood Sample Game

The Super Supreme Court has repeatedly validated the decisions previously handed down from the old Supreme Court: human genes may not be legally patented. #weconcur

That little commercial impediment, of course, hasn't stopped DJs from splicing signature "markers" into the code. Even if you can't collect intellectual property fees, you can still sell test kits that look through all the information contained in your blood just to find the one special "marked" gene they've discovered. Could be for muscular dystrophy, could be for immunity to smallpox. Could be for a connection to Henry VIII's offspring.

The test will tell you if you've got it. Or not.

Is it recreational? Is it medicinal? I don't know. Maybe both. I mean, these days, when girls have blood-testing bachelorette parties – *in old age, will I have perky boobs or saggers?* – it can be hard to tell.

If you've ever dabbled with these test kits – and, come on, who hasn't? – you know they can be an expensive addiction, particularly if you do one specialized search at a time. So if you're like me, then you start buying bundled kits, those blood-samplers that promise to test for three, or 12, or 100 different genes.

The Mapper™ is one of the biggest, like, 500-tests-in-one. There are probably bigger ones. They can tell you a lot about who you're going to be.

I used to check myself for various cancers, and other nightmare-causers. And, yeah, I admit I did the one that showed how many steps removed I was from the British Crown. Answer: *many*. Then, at some point, maybe after I started my job at the Agency, I quickly lost interest in testing my blood. I took a vow at the time to *live in the present* and not worry about future events I couldn't really control.

But that night when Marcy offered to do a complete mapping for me and Jonah, I became interested again. Without having to worry about costs – thank you publicly funded government materials – we could search for just about anything and everything. It was a lark. A game.

Marcy, before she left – and she did leave, without spending the night or anything like that – she instructed us to make a Top Five list. "Give me the five specific things you want me to look for. I can't find everything, of course. But there's more mapped out than you would imagine."

"So we can just…?" Jonah was trying to wrap his mind around the possibilities.

"You can just request whatever is most interesting to you," Marcy told us. "And if I can find it, I will. If I can't…you can pick something else." She smiled crookedly. Adorably.

"So, like, who I'm related to?" I asked.

Marcy nodded. "Yep. Like Magellan! Those are fairly easy. Some of the newer things – *traits*. Now, those are trickier. But I like figuring out tricks."

We all smiled at each other. It was intense.

Marcy explained that her current work was focused on identifying certain "trait" genes, the ones at the central core of our life narrative. Like: Are you wired to fight or to flee? Are you programmed to get a sexual thrill from violence or to feel nausea?

Are you going to spend your life desiring girls who look like boys or will you prefer boys who look like boys?

Or will you be wired to want both?

I was intrigued, and I said so. "Only five? Why are you so mean? I feel like I could make a list of, like, hundreds of things."

Marcy giggled. "All right. You can make your list ten. But I'm only going to have time to find five. But if I have some free time…"

I assured her I was kidding. "Five is fine. I'll play by the rules."

We agreed to send Marcy our lists by old-fashioned email. She could read them in the morning. For the sake of the game, Jonah and I compiled our lists separately, without the other's knowledge. Only when we shared them with Marcy would our choices be known.

At the time, it seemed like a harmless goof.

At the time, I didn't give it much thought. Maybe a few minutes while polishing my teeth before bed?

At the time, I think I was more focused on how hot the lovemaking was going to be with my JJ, now that we had spent a night together with Marcy, *in person*. I knew he was going to have plenty to say while I pleasured him. That's where my mind was at.

Now it all seems funny. Here's what I sent Marcy, about an hour after she left our place. This is a copy-n-paster:

Hey, Mar, great seeing you tonight! Thank you for being you – and for your generous offer of a super screening! Per your request, here's my world famous Top 5 Joan Galt Gene Searches...

1) Richard the Third of England, a highly successful BASTARD

2) President Maeve Bowden (why not?)

3) Stephen Hawking -- smartest dude *didn't know he had the ALS gene*. Different era. Anyway, I believe I may be related somehow. Easy to confirm/deny?

4) Gandhi (I know it's in the store kits; never checked!)

5) Famous Artists? [Long story really short: birth dad Theo Galt was an artist. Always wondered

where he got it and if I got. *Who's my daddy, Marcy?*[30]]

Jonah sent his in the morning, and we never discussed our blood samples in the interim. His mind was definitely elsewhere. #mmmmm

When I saw his list, I wasn't really surprised. I know my Jonah. [I LOVE YOU, BABE] Also, copy/pasted:

Dear Marcy,

With big thanks,

JJ

JONAH CHOICES

+ John Lennon

+ Bob Marley

+ Ghandi

+ Buddha

+ Is there a Compassion/Kindness gene?

Shortly after 9AM on Monday morning, Marcy sent us all a quaint "group email." She said most of our requests would be no problem – "pretty easy" she said.

---

[30] Attempt at a sexy joke. Epic fail!

And she wrote: "Joan: regarding #5…will do Raphael and Picasso to start. Jonah: regarding your #5…sort of! I'll see what I can do."

Marcy made it all seem like no big deal, certainly not a hardship. She said she'd even have enough time to do a couple of extras. "For both of you, I'm going to test for NELB14 (Cleopatra), because you two just seem to radiate her energy. ☺ And I'm also going to run you through the latest thing I'm doing. You're my lab rats! *LOL!*."

Jonah and I both textthoughted® our thanks and enthusiasm. This was going to be fun! We made plans to get together some time in the indeterminate future to chat about our amusing and amazing game.

And then I didn't think about my blood test again until Wednesday.

Now, I think about my blood test like every minute.

What Normal Looks Like

Looking back at my calendar for those two days, the Monday and Tuesday before my test results, I see the schedule of what seems to be a fairly normal girl living a fairly normal life. Check my feeds from those days, October 7 & 8; it's all archived (or should be, and probably will be until they start editing and erasing everything). You can tell my mind was in a totally different place, operating on a paradigm that seemed reliably solid.

I had no idea. I was oblivious.

Trust me, they'll have analysts scouring every second of my feed, piecing together the "clues." But I can save everyone the trouble: I had no idea.

Seriously. Have you looked? Here are the "highlights" from my exciting life:

MONDAY

+ Veggie power breakfast drink; took Pod to work

+ Reviewed Morning Briefing; reviewed Weekly Overview

+ Checked Inbox for updates: Got the Marcy email and quickly responded; got 14 invitations to future events, 11 of them tele- and 3 of them OIP. The Outdoors-in-person ones: my friend Janice's wedding [Sorry, girl! Won't be making it now. ♥ U]; 30th birthday bash for my good friend Joel, hosted by his husband, Wilson, scheduled for the next weekend; and a save-the-date for a New Year's Eve Y$1,000-a-ticket charity ball benefitting Lupus, held at the Smithsonian, hosted by the Embassy of China and sponsored by China Bank™. Responded to none.[31]

+ Worked

+ Lunch with Cassandra; received a Connection Alert® while standing beside a tallish, boyish girl near the raw juice bar; did not reply, but *did* announce the moment on my feed, along with a photo of my vegan quiche and steamed broccoli flowers

+ Checked Inbox for updates: Got 8 more invitations to future events, one of them OIP: a new music concert being given by friend Ashanti, collaborating with live birds. Didn't respond.[32]

+ Worked

+ At 2:22PM, got a salacious text from the Director; responded ambiguously; tweeted about it, calling him "Mysterious Stranger"

---

[31] I planned on doing that later, after consulting Jonah.
[32] Ditto.

+ Worked

+ Checked Inbox for updates: Got 3 more invitations, none OIP; got short sweet note from Jonah:

> Jo-Jo, my delicious vixen, how did I get to be so lucky to find you? Or did you find me? I was lost but now I'm found...LOVE YOU,
>
> YOURS, JJ

responded encouragingly; tweeted about it; read about newly discovered archeological scrolls from underneath what is now West Jerusalem that shows early and ongoing dissent between Moses and his disciples over the exact meaning of "Thou Shall Not Kill"; retweeted the story

+ Worked

+ Pod home; worked out; meditated; showered; tweeted about the calming fragrance of coconut in my artisanal shampoo

+ Dinner with Jonah; posted photos of our meal (protein patties; kale cookies) pre-candlight sim; discussed various invitations with him, jokingly suggesting he would really enjoy attending the Lupus Charity Ball with me; asked my network which OIP events I should attend; opened it to voting[33]

---

[33] Almost 62% voted for the Lupus Charity Ball, because then they'd get a photo of Jonah and me at the Smithsonian in formals – as if he would ever go to such a thing!

181

+ Vaporized; tantrasized; rated it all highly to recalibrate my algo-chip

+ Signed off

TUESDAY

+ Veggie power breakfast drink; took Pod to work

+ Reviewed Morning Briefing; reviewed updated Weekly Overview

+ Checked Inbox for updates: Got nothing from Marcy; got 9 invites, 2 OIP, one a coffee date with Megan and one another concert, featuring my friend Myrtle's retro band the Porky Pines; didn't respond immediately

+ Worked

+ Lunch with Cassandra and Jeff; shared photo of my vegan spareribs; received zero Connection Alerts® while loitering near the raw juice bar

+ Worked

+ At 2:03PM got a salacious text from the Director and, one minute later, one from Jonah; responded to both with "naughty boy!"; quick tweet about how nice it is to feel wanted

+ Worked

+ Checked Inbox for updates: More invitations, none OIP; old-fashioned emails from The Harvard™ (asking for money) and from Mother Elaine to let me know she was "thinking about" me and wishing that "our family" wasn't "so dysfunctional!"

+Pod home; worked out; meditated, showered; updated all feeds with "The root of beauty is cleanliness" and a photo of my hand on the shower knob

+ Dinner with Jonah; posted photos of our soy steaks pre- and post-grill; candlelight sim; discussed *his* work with the computer networking; discussed *his* plans for Wednesday, which included a meeting with Felix Zanger, the cyber-activist, and an OIP visit to a cricket farm interested in procuring his services

+ Vaporized; tantrasized; rated it all highly to recalibrate my algo-chip

+ Signed off

No meetings with shadowy foreign agents. No research at Jihadi Websites. No nothing. Just going about another day, and then the day after it, and fully intending on more or less doing the same thing the next day.

This is all 100% verifiable.

This part is *not* verifiable, but it's true, at least as far as I see it through my individual prism: My life was a nice life. I liked it. My life wasn't incredibly spectacular, but it wasn't boring, either. I was coming to terms with my past and confronting my present. I was adjusting. Letting go of my ego attachments. I was becoming a better person, or at least trying to.

I was happy. Not a million percent of the time, but happy enough.

I was also unconscious. I thought I knew.

I didn't know anything.

My blissful ignorance ended the next morning when I checked my Inbox.

Subject: Discussing Your Test

Subject: [Discussing Your Test]
Date: 11/09/2090 4:20:45 P.M.
From: Ilike2splice@G.com
To: JoJoGalt62@G.com

Dear Joan,

Please forgive the formality of an email. I didn't want to text this…

Some very interesting results in your blood test. (And Jonah's). I'd like to discuss ASAP – best OIP, I think. Are you free 2nite?

Please don't reply to my work address. You can zap me directly.

Sincerely,

Marcy Kim

When I first read the message, I remember being totally undisturbed by it. Marcy's tone seemed a little cold and distant, which bummed me a little, maybe. But she was like that sometimes, all professional and clinical. DJ at work.

Otherwise, I was, like, "Oh, 'very interesting' sounds very interesting." Which is how I replied to her, copying Jonah.

His whole attitude was basically: "Hmm. Interesting."

Yes, it was all quite interesting. This is a word you hear a lot. It means different things to different people. One woman's "dull" is another's "interesting." Another's "interesting" is *whatever* to someone else.

Here's something I've learned: you don't want your life to be *too* interesting.

There are moments, especially now, when I sincerely wish I could go back to my not-too-terribly-interesting life: work, friends, lovers, relationships. Taking the pod. Making dinner. Normal things. Dull things. Possibly even *uninteresting*, to me included.

They say you don't appreciate what you've got until it's gone. It's totally true. Since I joined the Termite Squad, I'm in a state of constant gratefulness.

The Grand Illusion

You know that feeling? The one you get when everything you *thought* you knew about someone turns out to be totally wrong? You feel sick, right? Like you're going to throw-up.

My friend Stacy had a nervous breakdown when she discovered that her husband of four years had been carrying on a torrid affair with their Burmese housekeeper slave -- for approximately four years. Like from the minute they got married. Whenever you tried to talk with her in the aftermath, pre- and post-divorce, it seemed like all she could say was, "I thought I knew him. I thought I knew the man I married. I didn't know him at all."[34]

Has this ever happened to you?

Has your whole conception of someone changed in one terrible instant? Until the sensation passes, you feel like your life is exploding, that you

---

[34] File under: Unadjusted Men Will Do Anything for *Katori* Action. #reality

can't breathe. All the beliefs that previously gave
you structure and meaning seem to be crashing and
crumbling.

You feel betrayed, fooled, exploited, used,
cheapened, and deeply disrespected. It's awful.

It's the worst, right?

Now, I want you to imagine that the person
you discover is not who you thought she was is…
yourself.

Marcy arrived at our place a little past
20:30. I remember thinking that was strange, since
she was famously punctual for everything. When
she joined us in our kitchen, where we were
upcycling our dinner remains, she declined our
good non-processed water, and she seemed to have
more difficulty than usual making eye contact with
me or Jonah. I may have even joked, "You sure you
don't need a hit, Marcy?"

She was all business. "So I got the results
from your blood tests, and as I mentioned, as I
wrote…there are some very interesting genetic
markers…both of you. Both of you have them."

Jonah asked, "Magellan?" He and I laughed.
It seemed funny to us. Marcy didn't really laugh.

"No, actually, neither of you," Marcy
reported, nodding.

For a second I felt super disappointed.
#irony.

"What I'm talking about is sort of
complicated," Marcy said, somberly. I looked at

Jonah. He looked at me. I could tell he was thinking what I was thinking.

"We're both sick?" I asked.

Marcy swallowed. "No, that's not what I meant."

"What's going on here?" Jonah asked, sounding mildly alarmed but still cool. "Just give it to us straight."

"We're not sick, Marcy?" I demanded.

"No, no…No, you're not going to get lung cancer in your thirties, or anything like that. You're fine. Really. No death sentences." She laughed mirthlessly.

"So what did you find?" Jonah asked calmly, now more intrigued than concerned.

"That's what I'm here to discuss." Marcy smiled then, and I could tell it was a fake smile, the kind you give to a young girl when she asks you why she doesn't have a mommy.

And then she told us.

She talked for what seemed like a long time. I'm paraphrasing the key parts. Jonah and I hardly interrupted or asked questions. We just listened.

Marcy said:

First, I just want to say I love both of you. Nothing changes for me. OK? I love who you are. I know who you are and I love who you are… I ran the complete work-up, with all the stuff you asked for in your top-five… No matches with anyone noteworthy. No Genghis Khan or Cleopatra.

Sorry... This is the interesting part. I was looking for the Picasso marker – OK, let me back up. You should know: we have a whole subset of genetic mapping and splicing that we currently file under the general heading of Artistic, *like the one that identifies rare musical talents. Or visual and spatial gifts. Right? So, specific artists, specific people, have their own codes, obviously, but* all *of them share a large percentage of the coding that falls under the general Artistic heading...To have the complete profile, with several key marker genes, is way more rare than you might assume. Like close to 1-in-a-million. Let me put that in perspective: You're more likely to have the Stephen Hawking, the ALS gene, than you are to have the Artistic profile...So, I was pretty amazed when I was looking around the mapping for Joan's last request, the Picasso and Matisse, and I realized that you, Joan, have the* entire *Artistic gene profile. Every one of them! You're not related to any famous artists that we currently have online, sorry, but it's definitely been passed to you by your parents. Possibly both but probably one. The odds are it's one...Anyway, I was pretty blown away to find this match in you, Joan. It's great! One of your parents was most certainly an artist, with the genes to make it happen. You seem to think it was your father. We can't say conclusively it wasn't your mother. But if your father exhibited artist signs – he did? So, yes, probably from him. But you got it, girl. The question, I guess is: What are you gonna do with it? Think about it...*

I remember feeling special, feeling like I was somehow touched by grace.

*So now I'm doing Jonah's list. Lennon. Marley.
Well, bits are showing up from both, but no direct
match to any of your requests, Jonah. But then – it's
weird, but in nucleotide terms, the profile for what
you asked for, the "Compassion" or "Kindness"
gene, is not actually one specific gene but a
complex profile of multiple genes, with some
incredibly rare markers mixed in. I assume from
your nods that you get it. Good! So this Compassion
profile is in many ways closely related to the
Artistic profile. Many direct correlatives. You could
say that Artistic is kind of discreet subset of the
Compassion profile, with a couple of super rare
golden genes added. Like the ones Joan has...So,
Jonah, I looked just a little deeper, on a hunch, and,
amazingly, you also have the complete Artistic
profile. Every gene. Yes! You're both like 1-in-a-
million people.*

We tried to digest this new information.
When I looked at Jonah, he seemed slightly
stunned, a little blown away, like he was still trying
to get his mind around it. He also looked mildly
skeptical (the way he usually does). And I
remember thinking at that moment – and this is
weird remembering it – I remember thinking,
"Maybe this revelation doesn't make Jonah feel
special because everyone already knows he's
special."

Me? I felt special. I felt elated. I felt I was
the me I had always known, but somehow different
and new. I felt like I wanted to immediately update
my feeds and tell the world.

I moved behind Jonah's Poschair™ and
gave him a soft hug, nuzzling my cheek against his

191

head, taking in his clean lavender smell, his good spirit. Marcy swallowed again and looked at the kitchen counter, as though it were her Armscreen.® She nodded, like she was assenting to an unseen questioner. Then she looked up and made herself smile.

Freshly composed, she continued.

The odds are pretty huge. So I looked deeper...You all know how DNA works? The protein chains? Meiosis? Alleles? You can check your arm later if you want all the jargon. I'll give you the main part. So in the current version of homo sapiens, including all the i-versions, we've got like around 3 billion base pairs of code. The next-generation hybrids a bit more, but let's say 3 billion. A large number. Now, most of us share 99.5% or more of the same genetic material. We're built with incredible similarities. We're all fundamentally the same machine. Except the reason we're not identical to each other is because of just a few nucleotides here, a few amino acids there. Mutations. Copying errors. Drift. And that's how each of us have literally millions of genetic differences among the billions we have in common...Now, in the case of twins – the duplication rate goes up. Especially in mono- zygotes, identical twins, obviously, but even they have some differences. I'm telling you guys this because...

Marcy stared at the kitchen counter again.

Like I said, I was blown away to discover that you both carry the Artist profile – that's just rare, super rare. It surprised me that you have so much genetic material in common. And in the course of testing both of you for the, I guess you could call it the

*special thing I'm looking at, my special project –
well, I was seeing so many similarities in areas that
are usually volatile, or what you would expect to be
highly dynamic, I kept comparing. I was intrigued...*

I still felt special at this moment. But the
way she kept staring at the tabletop. You could just
sense something wasn't right. I was standing behind
Jonah, gently massaging his trapezius, rubbing my
thumbs up his neck. He seemed tense.

*What I want to tell you is: the information is by no
means 100% totally conclusive. You know? This
could be a simple lab mistake. An anomaly...But if
it's not...Joan and Jonah, you two share a lot of
genetic material. A lot. Like 99.93%.*

Jonah's muscles stiffened beneath my
fingers. "You don't need a Sherlock app to deduce
that you mixed up the samples, Mar."

She nodded. "I know. I thought that, too. So
I re-tested. Twice. And also," she said, her voice
lowering, "your profiles aren't actually identical.
They're just very close to identical."

I blurted out, "Which means what exactly?"
I squeezed Jonah's shoulders. They felt like
grapefruits in my palms. He leaned back into me,
resting his taut head on my chest.

"What it would seem to mean, Joan, is that
you and Jonah are related."

My first reaction was: *So? Aren't we all?*
And then I was, like: *Jonah is a distant cousin, and
somehow through multiple foster homes and
adoptions we found each other. That's incredibly
romantic!*

193

"Related in what way?" Jonah asked, leaning forward. I could feel his whole back go tight.

Marcy made a couple of false starts. She dispensed disclaimers and caveats. And then she finally looked up and said, "I think you two share the same father."

Aftermath

I know you're going to look it up, try to find out. I'll save you the search. That was the night Jonah moved out.

We haven't seen each other face2face or OIP since then. And never will – unless he inexplicably shows up where I'll be when this is posted.

He and I never had "one last time." No gradual disengagement. Just a sudden ending.

Like a death.

That doesn't seem right to me. I understand why it has to be. Intellectually I get it. But my heart also understands what love really feels like – and my heart is broken. Utterly destroyed. And why? Think about it. Why should this be? How can love be wrong? In any form, how can LOVE be wrong?

I don't know. But apparently it can. Do you know how painful that is?

I'm not ashamed. Not disgusted. Not in any way. Not by our love, not by our lovemaking. Am I supposed to be? If I were, that would make some people happier. I'm sure that would pump up my stats – as if I really care. They want me to be all *I no longer could bear to look at him.* They want me to claim that *The thought of his hands on my naked skin made me nauseous.*

Sorry. Can't help you, Moralists.

I *ache* for Jonah. I miss him. You can call him whatever you need to call him, but it doesn't change the love he showed me. And, yes, the passion. #lovewins

But that night changed everything else. All my assumptions. It changed *me*. I had come so close to understanding myself, to filling in the blanks of my past, and now I had to start over. Rewrite the story. Because I had been looking for the wrong person. I wasn't who I thought I was.

For one thing, I wasn't an only child. That was a new concept.

There were questions ("Are you sure? Are you certain?") and crying and no doubt I raised my voice. Jonah did some uncharacteristic yelling.

Marcy was very calm and clinical, detached. I felt like I was suffocating. I couldn't get enough air into my lungs, couldn't draw enough breath through the piles of world that were crumbling on top of me. I may have fainted briefly, or had a spell of vertigo. My head wasn't right. My breathing off.

At first it was hard to look at Jonah. I admit the thought crossed my mind, *OMG, I've been sleeping with my brother.* But a bigger thought took over, *OMG, I've been* soulmates *with my brother.*

Jonah looked bad. Pale. Clammy. He went silent, inward. Gone.

I saw him and I cried. I knew I could try to go wherever he was, but I would never reach him. That's the part that ripped my heart open. I was overcome with waves of sadness, a lifetime's worth. 28 yrs. The love of my life was gone. He was here, he was alive. But the love, the *lover*, that I knew as Jonah Jones was gone.

We were destined to be just friends. Really good friends... *maybe.* And maybe this was the moment that I knew I'd lost him forever.

That was hard for me to accept. But I've learned to. I had to.

At first the pain was unbearable, the emptiness in all the places I used to fill with Jonah. The aloneness. It's true what they say about your WorthScore© and popularity totals: You can have millions of yuan-dollars or millions of friends and likers, but ultimately you're alone in the universe. You're on your own.

I didn't know if I could bear it. I consoled myself with a calming mantra: *This will all be over soon. This will all be over soon.*

Somehow that got me through it. *This will all be over soon.* I managed to survive that Wednesday night, and somehow the next day, and somehow the next night. And the next day, Friday, I woke up and realized what I had to do.

That's when I started writing this post. That's when I realized everything was going to be all right. The pain would end. The healing would begin.

I never felt dirty. I never felt our love was dirty. I never felt our love needed cleansing.

But I also knew I could make the world an altogether cleaner place.

More Aftermath

When Marcy had answered all his questions and showed him the math and the chemistry, Jonah said little. He seemed to be in a state of shock brought on by momentary confusion followed by profound disbelief. *WTF!* Of course, all I wanted to do was hug him. But when I went to put my arms around him in a comforting embrace, the kind we had shared every day since we fell in love, he pulled away and announced, "I think the best idea is for me to go. I don't want to…" He started to cry.

Then he turned and quickly left, taking nothing. I thought that meant he had to come back eventually.

"I think he doesn't want to cry in front of us," I mumbled to Marcy, and promptly broke into uncontrollable sobs. She also started to cry as she went to hold me, and I fell into her arms, grateful for the sanctuary.

"I'm sorry, Joan," she whispered. "I'm really sorry."

"It's not your fault," I sniffled, totally seeing how she could feel this was all her fault.

"I just hate to cause so much upset. That wasn't my intention."

"I know," I assured her. Marcy didn't want to split us up. She wanted to be closer to both of us.

"You're going to be fine," she cooed, calming me. "Everything will get better."

"Yes," I said. "Yes, everything will get better." And my breath began to return to me. My sobs trailed off, contractions lengthening. "Everything will get better."

"Yes it will. And, also, on the positive side, you have such an interesting profile. So many wonderful genes. You know, when I was looking –"

"Marcy, I'm sorry," I said, cutting her off. "I just don't think I can handle any more blood test talk tonight."

She said, "Of course. Some other time."

Too much weirdness. I couldn't handle it. I felt like I was about to lose it again, so I took a triple-strength Indicamax© drop, disconnected from all my feeds (incoming and outgoing), and switched to shut-down mode. Leaving a trail of clothes from the bathroom to the bed, I stripped to my undies. Marcy put me to bed, kissed me on the forehead, and let herself out.

I wanted her to stay. Just to hold me. To be with me. But it was probably for the best that she left.

The drops began to kick in, and I stared at
the darkening screen behind my eyelids. When it
went perfectly black, I could see a billion pixels, a
trillion pinpoints of LEDs gradually changing color,
uniformly flowing from purple to green to lavender
to yellow, and finally back to purple. All these
points of light. Little threads of energy, the structure
of the universe. I felt I was seeing into a distant
place.

And then I saw these words, written in the
sky of my mind, written in starlight:

Sacrificing your life for the benefits of
others is not a contradiction, because in
saving others your life becomes
precious and important.

I can see them today, just as vividly. At this
point I don't have time for theorizing about where
the message came from, or who the messenger was
or wasn't. God, the universe, whatever. The
important thing is that I got the message.

It was emblazoned in my mind, and I got the
message.

You can call me mentally dangerous, if it
makes you more comfortable. As you wish. But this
is not a *talking to an imaginary friend* thing. What I
experienced goes beyond the business of soul
saving.

I got a message from somewhere, let's call it
The Universe. And I'm just so happy and grateful
that I was able to hear it and understand it.

When I woke up that Friday, I felt a nascent peacefulness in my chest, the first time anything remotely like this sensation filled my heart since Jonah went incommunicado. I could *breathe* again.

I spent that day at work thinking about how everything I'm currently sharing with you could work, outlining my plan. I did it on old-fashioned paper, with an antique pen Elaine had given me.[35] Like a flowchart.

Without realizing it, three hours had passed and I hadn't checked my feeds once. It's hard to describe accurately, but the best way I can put it is: an unfamiliar lightness came over me. I felt like a weight had been lifted from my chest, and that a gloomy and cold place inside my core was now allowing in some warm beautiful white light.

On many levels I'm scared. I'm *so* scared. But in other ways, I'm not scared. I'm not afraid.

I am *not* afraid. I know that very soon my short visit to this planet will conclude. Maybe my soul will return in a different form, maybe it won't. No one knows.

Only one thing is certain: the world will be a better place when I'm gone.

---

[35] The paper was burned eventually. Anyone purporting to have an "original" copy is a fraud.

The Secret

Joanie Galt's Logistics Weekend. That's how I thought of it. Keep going. No pity parties. Fight the inertia! Move forward!

I tried to be positive.

So I spent the Saturday and Sunday following the blood test revelation trying to get my life arranged, or rearranged. I made lists. I thought encouraging thoughts and visualized encouraging images. I willed myself to not live in the past, a past I could never recapture and would never fully understand. I told myself to be in the golden present, where everything is beautiful, even when it's not.

And I tried to find Jonah. I reached out to his besties, Ferdy and those guys. I posted on a black site that only his friends would see. No response. No reaction. I assumed JJ had gotten to the Anons first, asking them to help him disappear. Radio silence. #hacktivistacollective[36]

---

[36] Hashtagged on purpose because that's one way

Did he tell them about his blood test? Did he tell them about me?

Did he mention Theo Galt?

I don't know. There's no feed traffic to search retroactively, and his network went mute. [Jonah, I know in my heart that you're reading this now – which is another way of saying I *know* that you're OK. And I sincerely hope that when this is over you'll still be OK.]

Talked with Megan. Talked with Cassandra. Talked with some other girlfriends. Didn't mention my test. Told them I was going through a thing with JJ, a serious thing – and would they let me know immediately if they heard from him? Or about him?

And I talked with Marcy. OIP face2face.

It was Sunday morning. At first we were texthoughting®, then after a few minutes she called me. I was looking at her concerned face on my arm, and I felt a powerful need to be hugged, to be held. It wasn't a sexual feeling. It was a need I guess I've had since I was little girl, a palpable hunger for protection and kindness and warmth. I blurted out, "Marcy, I think I really could use a hug right now."

I invited her to our unit. (*My* unit, I guess). While she got in the tube to come over, I

---

to guarantee they'll find and read this. I HAVE A BRIEF MESSAGE FOR YOU GUYS: I understand that you felt you had to protect JJ, but you did me wrong. And now maybe you can worry about something other than preventing me from talking to my brother.

straightened up the place, popped some Cloropellets™, and slammed a fresh hydrator. When Marcy arrived twenty minutes later, I greeted her at the door, willing myself to smile.

She was sporting the same tousled boy-hair and nerdy red shirt she had been wearing during our call. It was a lab blouse, with matching lab pants. "You look like you've been working," I said jocularly, trying to keep it light.

She stepped inside. "Come here," she said, opening her arms wide, beckoning me.

I moved into her embrace. And I'm not sure if I managed to hold back the tears until she had her arms around me, but I know they came quickly. I cried and cried, as though I'd finally been given permission to surrender. Marcy held me tightly. She was strong. I remember feeling profoundly grateful for her embrace. Relieved. Maybe even saved.

Forget about being made love to -- I hadn't been *touched* since Wednesday night, nothing more than a handshake at work. Breathing fitfully beside Marcy's neck – lemons and salt – it occurred to me that I hadn't had another human being's hands on my skin for four frighteningly lonely nights. It's so hard when every morning and every night of your life for the past three years has been filled with caressing and squeezing and petting, waking up to a beautiful naked man in your bed, always hungry for you – and then nothing…

When my breath returned to normal and I got my snotty face cleaned up, I tried my best to smile, and I said, "Thank you, Marcy. I needed that."

She said, "You're an extraordinary person, Joan."

I know she meant it as a compliment. At the time, it sounded more like, *"You're an extraordinary freak, Joan."* That was my mindset then. Very dark. I knew what I had to do, and I had a pretty good idea of how I was going to do it. But I hadn't yet found a way to be eternally happy about it.

I think I said something sarcastic, with a pronounced aftertaste of bitterness.

"I really mean it," Marcy said. "You're extraordinary. Look, my career is all about investigating Life, searching for where Life is designed and formed and built. I became a DJ because I had a fascination with the biggest mystery of all. You know how certain music or songs can get some people really excited? I get that way when I see certain gene maps. I get inspired when I see nature working the way the universe intended, spreading out the information in what *seems* like randomness but is actually an intelligent plan that we're only now starting to understand."

She held me by the shoulders and looked into my eyes. "And you've got one of the most extraordinary maps I've ever seen, Joanie."

That made me feel better. #notkidding

"You mean me and Jonah?" I thought out loud. "We've got the same map."

"Well, yes and no. I mean, yes. He's extraordinary, too. The Artistic profile – that's a gift, obviously. But how can I put this?" Marcy looked off into a corner of my apartment unit, where the crystals were hung. "He doesn't have what you have."

At first I didn't say anything. I just looked at Marcy's round face, her narrow eyes, her thin lips. She wasn't "beautiful" in any traditional sense (and I think Marcy would be the first to say so, without any weirdness). But I loved looking at her. And trying to read her.

She swallowed. I could actually hear it. And then she said: "Joan, do you remember that sequence I showed you the first time you visited my lab? I think you called it 'the parallelogram.' Well, that sequence is a gene I've been working on – and you know I'm not allowed to tell you for what purpose – I've been working on it for almost a year now."

I told her I remembered. It reminded me of our first kiss.

"Right. Well, it's officially called 47333-AR. That's its sequencing code. We've been, my team – we've been doing massive searches, enormous amounts of networked computing, trillions of tetra-gigs – and it's been mostly coming up trillions of misses."

Marcy's voice rose gradually. "You start to doubt it's actually out there, that maybe what you saw the first few times were explainable copying errors, anomalies within the standard variances. A big waste of time. Then you see it again, after all this looking, and when you *do,* when it's staring back at you, exposed and obvious, it seems perfectly clear that 47333-AR really *does* exist, that it's a brick in our human building blocks. It gets passed down through the generations, like all the other common genes. Hard to find, but *it's always there* in the background, waiting to mutate."

Marcy leaned her forehead in near mine, like she was going to kiss me.

"It's always there, but it's so difficult to see…And *that's* why I say you're an extraordinary person, Joan Galt." She pulled back to look at me. "Because you carry the gene."

How Can I Be of Service?

Daddy Michael and Daddy Peter always encouraged me to do whatever I wanted with my one and only life. They said they didn't care if I was a garbage collector or a federal judge – just so long as whatever I did I did as best as I possibly could. That was their philosophy: do whatever, but do it well.

That seemed like the way to go as a child, and as a teenager, and at The Harvard™. Find something you think is fun or interesting and go for it!

But now I see a different way. Instead of doing whatever we self-indulgently *want* with our life, what if we all identified the thing we could do with our life that would *be of optimal service* to our brothers and sisters, biological and otherwise?

What if we all were encouraged to discover our individual gift so that it could be properly cultivated and generously shared? With gene mapping being what it is, identifying the

Beethovens and McCartneys and Valerianos is easy. If you're not blessed with those chromosomes, then maybe you shouldn't pursue your dream of being an improvisational musician, no matter how much it appeals to you in theory. That would be a kind of misallocation of resources. If, however, you *are* touched, we've got a free conservatory waiting to help you grow your talent.

I didn't get any special talents. No gifts. In the grand cosmic lottery of random chaos, I was chosen to inherit 47333-AR.

I was given a curse.

Some of us are so afflicted. When you realize this is your fate, you ask yourself: how can I be of optimal service to my brothers and sisters, biological and otherwise?

The answer is clear. You do what I'm about to do.

Former Termite Tiffany Amber Liu's Game Plan?

My Termite Squad Application dossier, which I've managed to archive on several secure sites (for when they try to erase it), was pretty impressive. Everything was notarized and fingerprinted. Everything embossed on Sec-Pape™, with a verified algo-chip match. Everything very official.

Check it out: //JGaltTSApp/rkive4vr.com.

My diagnosis: born with AR-47333 and infected by UID, unintentional incest disease.

My *other* diagnosis, which required less explaining – Stage IV breast cancer, spreading to lymph, lung, and brain.

I had my cancer verified by three different oncologists. I was terminal, they said. They estimated I had three-to-four months to live.

That was about two months ago, so it seems that the doctors were right.

I'm not about to implicate anyone, so no names. Just want to say that it's totally true: with enough money you can buy *anything*. In the case of fake medical certificates, it's not actually a money issue. They're not that expensive.[37] It's a *connections* issue. You've got to know the right people.[38]

I knew the right people.

And I don't mean only to procure authentic looking fake documents. I knew *PWRS*. My whole family on my mother's side is comprised of PWRS. Every one of them a difference-maker.

Would I have been approved for the Termite Squad without my "special" relationship with the Director of Operations? I don't know. My "keep the ladies, add the sexy" angle really seemed to resonate. Also – and I don't care how bad it sounds – when he discovered that it was *me* who wanted to break the age-barrier, *me* to be the first Termite under 100, I bet he was relieved. He knew he

[37] Around Y$1,000 each.

[38] Like everything else, right?

wouldn't have to explain anything to his estranged spouse. His inconvenient mess would be all cleaned up.

God, I hope the world is reading this right now! #transparencyisabitch

Of course, that's not what he said when I showed him my documents. No, he made the appropriate noises of regret and dismay. He was "so sorry" and was taking it all very hard.

The Director asked me, "Are you sure about this, Joan?"

"Never more sure," I replied. "I'm prepared to be a Termite. I'll be proud to be a Termite."

He looked over my papers. He shook his head regretfully. "I don't want to let you go." He got up from behind his desk to embrace me, but I stepped back and extended my hand.

"That's over. It's all over," I said. "We're done."

He said he understood, but I could see a familiar lasciviousness in his gaze. "I understand. I just wish I could comfort you somehow." He stepped toward me.

"Make this easy for me," I said, suddenly feeling very emotional, like I was going to cry.

"Yes. Sure. Of course," he stammered. "Whatever we can…" He wrapped himself around me and hugged me enthusiastically, especially my ass.

I extricated myself and looked him in the eye. "I'm dying, you pig. I'm dying *for my country*. So show some respect."

In less than 48 hours, they approved me for probationary inclusion in the Termite Squad. #howshitworks

I moved out of my windowless office. I was instructed to report to another office – a conference room – in the basement of the innermost ring at the Pentagon. My service was to commence immediately, time being of the essence.

Orientation, briefing, training – it all happens rapidly, usually because qualified candidates have a looming expiration date. Turnaround (from approval-to-Termite-to-monument-inspirer) is typically one month or less.

At mine, I attended boring in-person meetings, the face2face kind, with bland men in shirtsleeves, their Armscreen™ exposed, many of them sporting ironic facial hair. A guy named Mike was my lead "Coach."[39] He confessed that I was his

---

[39] Never gave me his last name. Not pertinent, it seemed at the time. I'm sure someone will figure it out eventually.

youngest ("Obviously!") and that it was a little…?
He couldn't find the word.

"Weird?" I proposed.

He laughed nervously and nodded. And with
the general state of weirdness duly noted, we
commenced.

The "training" was simplistic: how to adjust
the straps on your Endvest™, how to talk with your
handler through the radio implant, how to smile.[40]

The Coaches seemed to be accustomed to
dealing with women of highly reduced mobility, not
athletic go-getters. The underlying message of all
the orientation, addressed to the wheelchair crowd:
just be ready to snap the switch, we'll do the rest.

The magic switch. It's located on the bottom
of the vest, near the waist. For safety reasons, it
requires two-hand fingerprint verification *and* a
unique up-and-to-the-side motion to engage, not
just a physio-match.

There was a ridiculous amount of practice
with the switch. They wanted all Termites to get
that part right. #click!

Maybe because I had more functional brain
cells than the sisters who came before me, I found
the practice sessions incredibly depressing. You
realize: *this* is the last thing I'll ever do.

Up and over to the side.

For the first couple days of my Termite
Squad orientation I was bored, anxious, and

---

[40] "Happy ladies earn more trust!" they told me.

miserable. It's not that I had second thoughts...I already knew my target, whomever was eventually chosen, would be a righteous one – not like some of the unlucky souls on the Kill List. I already knew my death wouldn't be in vain. I knew what the end would bring...but I was still in a very dark place, filled with anger at invisible forces that were way too large for me to fight.

After a while I was gradually fed more practical information – how close you have to be to ensure 100% success (8 feet; best if you can make out eye color, assuming you can still see through your Centurion cataracts). How to accept a handshake *and* activate the switch (use both hands; get the target to lean in).

The days seemed to accelerate. I decided to write this document about two weeks ago, around December 15th. I knew there were going to be questions and I wanted to be the one answering them, not my handlers. I consider it part of "getting my affairs in order," which all Termites are encouraged to do.

During Holiday Week (December 24-30), the week leading up to my impending ship-out date (location Top Secret and known only to the Director at that point), I was told to prepare for a simulation. "An actual simulation," is what they called it.

On the 29th, at the end of the day's training session, Coach Mike pulled me aside. "Please familiarize yourself with this tonight," Mike said, handing me this document, scanned for your convenience and uploaded to the usual archive sites.[41]

---

[41] I'm fully aware that to those who hate me and

You're welcome. I say this with all humility,
the kind of humility leakers and whistleblowers
everywhere ought to exhibit. We're merely
messengers trying to be the change we wish to see.

---

what I stand for, posting this document will
confirm my treasonous character. Some things, I
believe, are not meant to be kept secret.

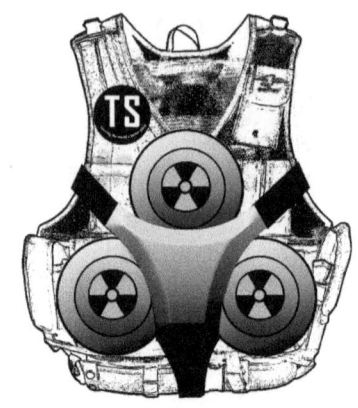

TOP

SECRET

FOR USE SOLELY AS A TRAINING TOOL IN PREPARATION FOR TERMITE SQUAD SERVICE

A SAMPLE ACTION PLAN

[NSA Waiver Status: Material compiled from Approved Theoretical Documents and pre-cleared Approved FTSD Training Documents; Form 507ESR on file.]

Dear Future American Hero,

Thank you for your service to the people of the United States of America and the principles we treasure. You are an important soldier in the War Against Evil. We salute you!

In 72 hours or less, you will be collected at your pre-arranged pick-up site by members of the Termite Squad Transportation Team. **You will not need to bring anything with you except:**

+ **essential medications** (anything you *must* take to stay alive for another 12-24 hours; otherwise don't bring your pills)

+ **your favorite blanket or plush toy**

All other items will be supplied for you, such as snacks, hydrators, fresh undergarments, amusements and commemorations. Your custom-measured wheelchair[42] and Endvest™ will be held on or near your mission site.

---

[42] Further evidence that this is a form letter. Never any talk of me using a wheelchair. We even discussed having me *dance* with the target.

Per Termite Squad training, upon pick-up your Armscreen™ will be disabled and all communication with anyone but your Coach will end. **Your family will be notified immediately upon successful completion of your service.** All benefits to which they are entitled begin accruing upon the first of the month following your successful service.

If you are unable to understand instructions at the time of your pick-up, whether because of auditory or comprehension issues, **you will be assigned a Termite Squad Communications Specialist** who will be authorized to speak on your behalf.

Per your training, **your main responsibility is to engage your vest switch.** Any required maneuvering or repositioning of your chair will be managed by a Termite Squad Valet, who should always be addressed as "my helper."

After pick-up **do not speak with anyone except your Coach.** If you are approached by a stranger or law enforcement authority, act confused and allow your Termite Squad Valet to intervene, per your training.

Although every Termite Hero is assigned a unique mission based on her physical fitness and American foreign policy objectives, **most missions are designed to follow the same general outline**. Knowing what's coming next can bring real peace of mind, so please review the following Mission Outline, which addresses many FAQs.

SAMPLE MISSION OUTLINE[43]

02:00 hours EST: TERMITE HERO PICK UP. Entry through front door. Egress through back door.

02:05: TERMITE HERO SECURED IN GROUND TRANSPORTER. Termite Squad Communications Specialist inside transporter.

02:12: TERMITE HERO ARRIVES AT HELICOPTER. Termite Squad Valet wheels Hero to helicopter.

---

[43] I have no evidence to confirm or deny that this Mission Outline was based on the actual Mission Outline for Termite Tiffany Amber Liu – TAL on any Termite chat forum – who was one of the so-called "pioneer Termites," one of the first three women to successfully serve their country. But a slightly different (very slightly IMO) version of this Mission Outline has already turned up on some black sites. Authentication impossible.

02:15: TERMITE HERO SECURED IN HELICOPTER. Communications temporarily halted because of noise; Termite Squad Communications Specialist on hand.

02:20: TERMITE HERO ARRIVES AT AIRFIELD. Termite Squad Valet wheels Hero to airplane.

02:25: TERMITE HERO SECURED IN AIRPLANE. Medical Monitors onboard. Comfort Givers onboard. Wheels up! Food, drinks, and pillows provided.

07:15: LAST MEAL SERVED. Per your custom menu. Intravenous option available.

08:45 (approx.)[44]: TERMITE HERO ARRIVES AT DESTINATION. Transfer to ground transporter.

08:48: TERMITE HERO SECURED IN GROUND TRANSPORTER. Switch Hero to custom chair, outfit with Endvest™. Radio check. Final affirmation confirmed by Termite Squad Communications Specialist.

09:18 (approx.): TERMITE HERO ARRIVES AT DESTINATION. Termite

---

[44] Many people think this is the giveaway that it's TAL's M.O. The flight time! Almost exactly the distance from her East Coast base to Caracas.

Squad Valet wheels Hero to Entry Door. Vest engaged and armed.

09:22: TERMITE HERO IN POSITION. Termite Squad Valet exits building, enters ground transporter, and confirms safe location with Hero's Coach.

09:25-?: SURVEILLANCE TEAM MONITORS TARGET. Termite Hero holds favorite blankie or teddy.

+ When Target is in range of Hero, Coach delivers code message: ***Termite time! With liberty!***

+ All Heroes are advised to reply audibly and clearly: ***And justice for all!***

[Time To Be Determined]: TERMITE HERO ENGAGES SWITCH. Two hands. Up and to the side. *In case of switch failure, vest will be activated by remote manual override.* Termite Squad service completed.

We thank you for keeping your grateful fellow citizens safe from harm. You will always be remembered and celebrated.

On behalf of the American People,

With Tremendous Gratitude,

YOUR FRIENDS AND COLLEAGUES AT THE TERMITE SQUAD

I haven't gotten my personalized Mission Outline yet. Supposedly that's coming tomorrow – which means that the day after tomorrow is probably my Target Date.[45] So I need to get this all wrapped up and reviewed and archived pretty quickly. Forgive me if this starts to sound rushed. Some of us are busy getting ready to explode. #joke?

Obviously, the Mission Outline they're going to give me will be a little different than the standard, since I don't think they're planning on putting me in a chair. But reviewing TAL's M.O. has been super helpful to me. It's reminded me about certain precautions I'm going to need to take. Because it's pretty obvious to me that whether or not the Termite pulls her switch, they can activate your vest remotely.

That's how I read it. You're basically an IED on wheels, with a nice smile.

Good to know. Reviewing TAL's Mission Outline has calmed me. Given me peace. It's helped me see how my conception of a truly noble Termite service is totally possible.

Now I think I know how I'm going to do it.

---

[45] *So* strange writing that. The finality.

Goodbyes

The clock is ticking for all of us, from the moment we take our first breath. For some of us the final alarm rings earlier than we might have planned or wished. That's just the way it is – and no, I'm not being all callous about it. Anyone who thinks she's entitled to a long life probably didn't grow up in a slave state, or anywhere else where they don't have proper nutrition, education, and water. Some of us are randomly selected to have nice lives; some to have crappy lives; and some of us are destined to have a short life.

Yes, I'm bummed, on one shallow level. But everything will be OK, and whether or not I, the girl they called Joan Galt, daughter of Theo Galt and Elaine Barclay Huxley, inhabits planet Earth in the year 2091 (or beyond) is irrelevant to the universe.

The fact that I'm *gone* is what's going to matter.

I don't have time for sentimentality. Sure, I'll miss sunrises and sunsets, and the moonlight, and the feel of cool sand between my toes and ocean breeze in my nose, briny and alive and eternal. I'll miss poetry and music. And birds. I could make a whole list.

That's not important now.

Neither is saying individual goodbyes. Don't be mad at me if I didn't texthought® U! I still love you. *I thought about you.* Daddy Michael and Daddy Peter, I love you so much!

All my friends, all my likers, please understand: This long rambling post is my goodbye to *all of you.* I'm addressing it you, specifically. Imagine me saying your first name before you read it. I'm saying, "[Your Name], I'm bidding farewell to you and I'm explaining as thoroughly and honestly as I can WHY this had to happen."

If I start saying farewell to all the people and the places and the experiences and the feelings and the sensations I'm going to miss…well, I'll never stop. And then this report wouldn't get finished in time. In which case you wouldn't know the truth about the 47333-AR gene.

That would be a shame, not getting to that part. Because it's the main reason why we have to say goodbye.

A Gift from My Mother

Jonah and I have the same father, Theo Galt.

Jonah and I have different mothers. Elaine Huxley is mine; his unknown.

Jonah doesn't carry 47333-AR, actively or recessively. I'm active.

Do the math. It seems pretty obvious who gave me the gene, right?

Elaine, of course.

That's what I thought.

When I announced my assumption to Marcy, there in my apartment, in the time-standing-still moments following her "you're such an extraordinary person" revelation, she scrunched up her face, like she was sorry, like she had to explain to a young orphan girl the truth about where the little waif really came from.

"Joanie, it's not really that simple." She explained the science to me then, in my kitchen, actually. You can check your arm if you want to learn all the terminology. I'll boil it down: in order to have anything like statistical certainty -- within one standard deviation -- you need to test the DNA of *both* parents. Otherwise it's just highly educated guessing."

She bit her lip. "You would have to get samples from both sides…which, even if you were somehow in touch with your mother…"

"I am!" I told her.

"And she would give you…Could you get a DNA sample from her?"

"Yes!" I replied, not worrying about the logistics. It couldn't be that hard. One of our lunches. Lipstick on a glass or something.

Marcy nodded and shrugged a little. "That would be a start," she acknowledged. "But, I hate to be a bring-down, Joanie…You know, even with a full analysis of your mother's map the results aren't going to be remotely conclusive unless we also did a map of your father. And unfortunately it's too late for that."

"Why?" I said, hearing something like pleading creeping into my voice. "Why not?"

"Well, because – I thought you said he died. When you were an infant, a child…"

I nodded silently, defeated.

Marcy tried to console me. "I mean, it's a super longshot at this point, but maybe if your mother, or somebody, anyone -- if someone kept

some personal effect of his, something we could
dust or scrape…you never know."

"Like what?" I asked. "Like an old book of
his?"

"Possibly," Marcy replied unenthusiastically.
"But unless he managed to bleed on it, or spit…"
She frowned apologetically. "We sort of need
organic material. Proteins."

That's when it all came together. When
Marcy mentioned proteins. I was propped on my
elbows, with my head in my hands. My fingers
were in my hair, pressed on my skull, like I was
trying to knead a good thought out of my scalp.
When she said "proteins" I happened to be touching
my hair – and for some reason I was reminded of a
memory from my childhood. It was elementary
school. Potomac Friends. I was maybe 10. This was
still during my "quiet child" period. Our teacher, a
dour woman who'd been teaching remedial science
for a long time, was talking about how hair grows.
Just the night before, I had overheard a conversation
between my two dads about someone's hair. I heard
them frequently using the word "nerve" or "nerves,"
and I somehow got it in my youthful mind that the
hair on our heads was actually made from dried
nerves. Like, they just sort of sprouted and dried.
Which is why hair was so thin. I don't know what I
thought. I just had it in my brain that hair was
composed of nerves. Having been strongly
encouraged to speak up when I thought something
was wrong or unclear, I raised my hand, right in the
middle of our teacher's lesson. This was
uncharacteristic behavior for me; she noticed right
away. "Yes, Joan?" she said, and I could tell by the

look on her face that she wasn't mad or anything, just surprised.

Using confident-sounding phrases that I'd heard adults use, I said, "Pardon me. Correct me if I'm wrong, but aren't hairs, human hairs, aren't they nerve endings?"

I saw the teacher's face change to an expression of vague bewilderment. "Like dried nerves?" I proposed, suddenly feeling inconsolably foolish. I could already tell I was totally wrong. "No, Joan. You're mistaken," the teacher said flatly. "Hair is *protein*."

Since then, I've been acutely aware of this fact.

I felt a pleasant jolt run through me, like when the vapor first hits you, or the moment you get aroused by the smell of a new lover. My eyes felt moist. The skin on my belly and my chest started to tingle. I snapped up out of my chair and looked around my kitchen.

I saw the wooden knife holder behind Marcy, near the sink, with the blades safely sheathed in their slots, organized from thick (butcher's knife) to thin (fruit paring knife), with their butt ends sticking out. I moved toward it, my eye already trained on the one I wanted.

"What are you doing?" Marcy asked, mildly alarmed. I didn't waste time explaining.

"This should do," I announced, tugging the antique sharpening rod from the block. I held up the long, solid steel cylinder – which I'd used hundreds of times to sharpen blades the old fashioned way, without lasers. It makes a horrible metallic screech, but you get knives that could make suicide relatively painless. This antique sharpening rod, I've discovered over the years, also comes in handy for cracking ice into small pieces, or anything else that needs a good *whap*!

I strode to the far wall. Without allowing myself any time to consider the ramifications, without giving myself time to consider how much it was going to hurt, I smashed the steel rod into the glass case containing my father's *accumulation*.

It shattered instantly, cascading to the floor like a loud rain. I reached inside, hit by a whiff of old air, of mold and heat.

"Here you go. This should do," I said, pinching out with my nails a few dry black threads of Theo Galt's 35-year-old glue-mounted hair.

The Termite Squad:
My Official and Authentic Report

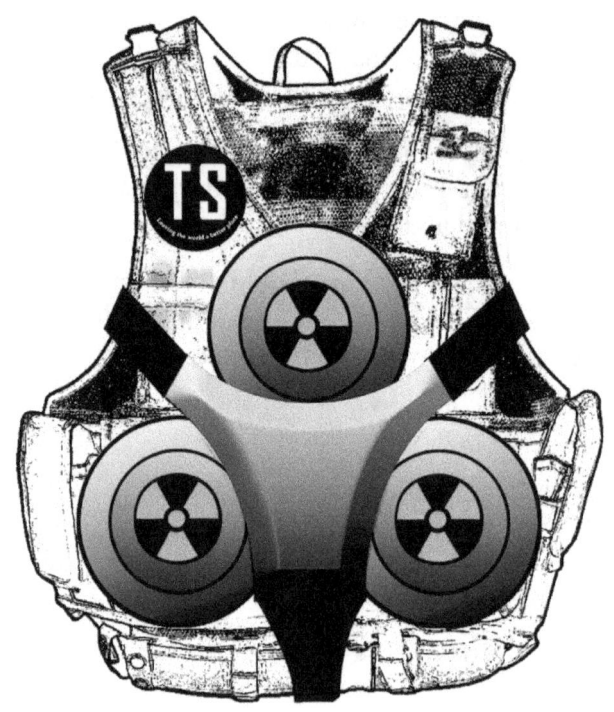

Let Me Ask You Something?

Real simple question. Please vote your answer. Would be nice to know where the world stands on this issue, at this point in our history.

Q: Which would be more likely to inspire you to kill yourself?

Answer 1☐ Finding out you've been having incredibly passionate multi-orgasmic sex with your brother.

Answer 2☐ Finding out you carry 47333-AR.

The Mark of an Extraordinary Person

When Marcy kept insisting on how extraordinary I was, I knew something bad was happening. I could feel I was being sold something. In this case: *you're not a horrible freak, you're so* special. *Your differentness is wonderful, not weird!*

"Joanie, please, listen to me," she said, holding me by the shoulders again. "It's truly extraordinary, by every definition of the word, it's extraordinary for someone to have the kind of map you have. Artistic *and* 47333-AR. I mean, I know dozens of very bright people who are going to want to study you."

We'd raced to her lab, where she hand-cultured a sample from Theo's ancient hair and express processed the analysis by linking to some

[46] This was pretty late at night; maybe even very early the next day, before dawn. Lots of unused brains.

dormant networks.[46] And just to be safe, for conclusive back-up, she slammed through another sample of one of my hairs, too. It seemed like the whole thing took less than an hour.

When the results starting displaying on her wall monitor, side-by-side, Theo's on the left and mine on the right, Marcy went off in search of the parallelogram marker, tapping furiously at her keyboard. She looked determined, fierce. I remember thinking, *that's wonderful, that look.*

It didn't take her long. "Got it!" she announced. "There." I stared at the monitor as she zoomed onto my map, the one on the right. "Confirmation. That's 47333-AR."

Yes. It was obvious. Anyone could see it if they knew what to look for.

I definitely had it.

She switched over to Theo's map, zooming to the pertinent region, where the parallelogram was located in my sample. You could see many shapes. Triangles mainly, some long rectilinear box-like things. But nothing you would immediately recognize as a parallelogram. Marcy grumbled, "It should be right around here...let me..." She pulled back slightly, scanning wider. Then she started to hum audibly, low short tones. Not sure if she was aware that she was doing it. Very concentrated girl.

Finally, Marcy sighed loudly and said, "Your father wasn't a carrier."

"No?"

"No. The chromosomal markers are definitely not present in this sample. So if this is actually his hair –"

"It is," I insisted.

"Then we can easily determine that the person whose head this hair sample came from definitely didn't carry 47333-AR."

"Which means?" I asked.

"Which means that you got it from your mother."[47]

Look, I really don't know how to explain this part other than to just basically admit that I guess all along deep down I knew. I *knew* that this had to come from Elaine Barclay Huxley. I knew it.

I knew this was why Jonah didn't have it. Theo may have been his dad, but Elaine wasn't his mother.

Deep down I had an unconscious understanding of what the Galts had given me and what the Barclays had given me. I could just smell it somehow.

So when Marcy broke the news, it was really almost like one of those déjà vu moments, where you've already been there and you already know how everything turns out. I take this as a sign that it really is possible to enter the 15th dimension

---

[47] This has subsequently been confirmed conclusively by two separate tests on clean samples.

and do some time-surfing, to skip back and jump ahead, all in an instant.

The Galts gave me my Artistic profile. #irony

The Barclays gave me 47333-AR. #bummer

"Well, that's all settled," I said, way too cheerily. I wasn't freaking out or anything. I was more like, "This all makes sense. Not a big deal."

But Marcy thought it was actually a very big deal. This is when she launched into her *you're-so-special* pep talk.

Ah, yes, I'm so very special. Special me. I'm artistic! Or more formally: Artistic profile. That's pretty special. Yay for me.

But a lot of people have that profile. Not by percentages a lot, but overall gross numbers. There's a lot of human beings on this planet. So I guess it depends on how you define "special." Like, how few people have to be a certain way for it to seem *special*, and not just "uncommon"? It comes down to what's your definition of *rare*.

Mine is this: If less than .01% of 1% of the population – the proverbial *one in a million* – carries a chromosomal marker, that's rare.

What do you think? Is that rare?

Let me ask you this: If only .01% of 1% of the population were born with Armscreens™ and never needed implants, would you think they were rare?

I would.

If one-in-a-million were naturally born with a third eye, would you think they were rare?

I would. Because 1,000,000 is a giant number. Start counting now, out loud. 1-2-3-4-5…See how long it takes you to get to 1,000. A *loooooong* time. Then imagine doing that 1,000 more times. That's what one-in-a-million feels like.[48]

When .01% of 1% of the population has *anything* it's rare. Something strange is happening. Something off. Something contrary to the rules of random distribution.

Something wrong.

When .01% of 1% of the population has the vast majority of the population's wealth, something is *wrong*. Those that can find reasons to disagree with this obvious conclusion tend to be one of those divinely blessed one-in-a-million.

People like my Uncle Jason and Uncle George. People like Uncle Warren Singh and his revered offspring.

People like me.

Yes, I carry the same diseased genetics as them. But it doesn't mean that I think slavery is good. It doesn't mean that I'm willing to perpetuate the illness. We may share 99.99% of the same genetic material, me and my uncles, but it's that last little .01% of 1% that counts. The *one-in-a-million* difference.

---

[48] Or you could start counting the words in this overlong post! They add up to about 3% of 1,000,000, so you'll be at it a while.

Comforting thought: *Maybe I'm special,
after all.* In this strange way. This difference. This
ability to see *who I really am.*

My theory is that under normal
circumstances, when mitigating factors like an
Artistic profile aren't present, when there's nothing
to calm the inflammation, those afflicted with
47333-AR are programmed to be oblivious to the
unnaturalness of their existence. They just can't see
it.

They can't see how harmful it is for so few
to hoard so much at the expense of so many. Even
when presented with heartbreaking evidence –
video feeds, even -- they're *not able* to see the harm
that hoarding causes. They can't do it. Empathy has
been bred out of them. They're hardwired to be
sociopaths.

They're hardwired for greed.

They truly can't help themselves. Maybe
somewhere in their subconscious they wish they
could, they wish they were able to control their
compulsion. But they won't, because they can't.
This goes beyond willpower and intention. You
can't tell your genes what to do. They tell you.

We all do what we can.

I praise the universe and say I AM
BLESSED that I was given enough countervailing
hardwiring to know the difference between right
and wrong. Unlike most people who carry 47333-
AR, I can discern the cost of my genetic flaw.

And it's intolerable.

The cost in human suffering is intolerable. The cost in animal suffering is intolerable – and not just the mass incarceration of nutritious insect species. *All* living creatures suffer because of 47333-AR carriers. The earth suffers. Nature suffers. The environment and the atmosphere. Everyone and everything pays the cost and bears the burden so that the .01% of 1% can fulfill their genetic destiny to eat the world.

I'm infected, but I can recognize this. How very special, indeed.

You normal people – and by now you've been tested, right? – you don't have a constant fear of not having enough, of somehow running out. Sure, you occasionally, maybe even *frequently,* worry about money, or potable water, or your Liker count. You may fret about it a great deal. *But you don't live every second of your life in mortal fear that someone else will have more than you.* Every now and then you're able to see that *there's really plenty for everyone.*

You may never be one of the PWRS, you may never have much of an impact on millions of strangers you'll never meet, but yet you know that somehow it's all going to be just fine. There's plenty for everyone.

If we share and make nice, there's plenty for everyone.

You do feel that, right?

The very special, super extraordinary achievers who carry 47333-AR *never* believe there's plenty for everyone. That's why they need more for themselves.

That's why we fight, why we make wars and torture our fellow humans as though they were 20th Century livestock. That's why so many must suffer. Because a few are programmed to believe they need more.

In the paper age, whole books used to be written about how the planet's problems all come down to poor distribution. I'm sure I read some of them in college. The idea is pretty simple: there's no shortage of anything in this world, except compassion. We don't have a scarcity of resources; they're just distributed very badly.

Some people have more than they need of something (water, oil, crickets) and some have less than they need of something (water, oil, crickets). The marketplace and commerce, fuelled by self-interested actors, are supposed to take care of getting stuff spread out properly, and sometimes they do.

But in the case of wealth – expressed as money and real estate and tangible assets – wealth is *never* distributed properly. It's not that we as a society, a civilization, a species, don't have enough wealth to go around so that every single living creature, every human and every animal, can have a dignified and peaceful existence here on this magnificent green planet. We have plenty. But the majority of that planetary wealth is held in the covetous hands of a genetically damaged few.

The 47333-AR gene predisposes the carrier to hoarding, especially of power and wealth (which are essentially the same thing these days). I can easily guess why our government is investigating the splicing possibilities, and I'm sure you can, too.

242

[IMPORTANT NOTE FOR INVESTIGATORS: *Marcy never told me what the Agency planned on doing with her research; I'm just exercising my constitutional right to infer.*]

If you have the gene, you're certainly not guaranteed to become a billionaire. But according to the data, you're guaranteed to have 47333-AR if you're a billionaire. It's like an essential amino acid in a certain type of person. Tycoons, oligarchs, dictators – the PWRS of PWRS and kings of kings.

What science is starting to understand – thank you, scientists, for seeking Truth, like Eddie Glass! -- if you have it, along with all your riches you also inherit the toxic byproducts that go with it. She who carries the gene is constantly at war with herself.

She has to fight the impulse, triggered, according to Marcy, *at birth,* to have more of everything – even when it means that everyone else will have to make do with less.

She has to fight the impulse to find herself the most interesting and valuable being in the universe.

She has to fight the impulse to put her needs and desires above all other concerns.

The impulse to seek personal comfort and convenience instead of universal dignity.

The impulse to cheat, steal, rape, ravage, and conquer everything she touches. *That's* the struggle of the 47333-AR carrier.

I can already foresee the comments at the bottom of this post, hundreds of pages of them: *Joan Galt was obviously consumed by self-loathing.*

Just another self-hating orphan...

Joan Galt let her inner fears get the best of her...

Folks will say what they will. I can't control that – other than by disabling public comments.[49]

But I can make my position perfectly clear, so there's no interpretive chicanery: I don't hate myself.

I DESPISE WHAT I'M BOUND TO BECOME.

---

[49] Which I'm not about to do. This is supposed to go viral, not private.

Actual Simulation

HISTORY MARKER: *It's about 18:45 on December 30.*[50] *I'm texthoughting® this in my unit, and I'm trying not to focus on the fact that this will be the last night I sleep here. Or anywhere. I need to make a record of what happened today. I think it will be incredibly useful for anyone wanting to understand what's going to happen tomorrow.*

This morning I went in for my "actual simulation," the dress rehearsal for tomorrow's mission. It was an intense day.

When I arrived, after swiping in and enjoying a pass through the Termite Hero's buffet (laid out exclusively for me, basically, since I was supposedly the only Termite being prepped), I told Coach Mike I had reviewed Tiffany Amber Liu's Mission Outline – "the sample outline," he corrected me – and that I really didn't have any questions. Except one.

---

[50] Time-stamp verified.

"Sure. I'm here to answer all your questions," he replied, smiling at me as though I were 106 years-old.

"Mike, I read it all pretty carefully – am I correct? Your Termites don't really have to activate the switch? That you have redundant systems in place?"

At first he chuckled and didn't answer. I let my question hang in the silence. "I think, yes, that would be correct," he finally stammered. "Redundant systems? We have – yes, the mission has safeguards built in."

"That's what I thought," I said, staring at him, daring him to look me in the eye. I knew he couldn't.

Mike didn't look me in the eye the entire day. He knew I knew: The Termite Squad is just a collection of hyper-controlled, precisely positioned bombs masquerading as adorable old ladies.

They can blow us up from a safe distance. We're human drones.

That's good to know, I thought. My mission could be terminated sooner (or later) than planned. Without my consent.

Do you understand now why I can't post this until, like, *seconds*, before I complete my service? If they got even the slightest advance notice…*kaboomskies*.

I was instructed to go with an Assistant Coach named Melanie to the Outfitting Department. She had an iris screen *and* cyber-glasses. Generic haircut and clothes. That's all I remember about her.

We walked down the hallway silently, blissfully free of small talk about nothing. Free also of big talk about subjects none of us is comfortable discussing out loud. I think the Termite Assistants are trained not to ask questions of the Termites, and it's probably for the best.

Melanie led me into artificially sunlit room cluttered with Kelpfoam™ and fabric. In the corner, mounted on a mannequin molded to my precise coordinates, was the most stunning little black dress. Accessorized with saltwater free-range pearls. I knew it was for me, but I didn't want to assume.

Then I was instructed to put it on.

I was guided to a spare changing area, behind a screen. I was told to hang my "civilian clothes" on the rack inside, and to leave my shoes behind as well.

I stripped to my bra and thong. "Ready," I called out. The outfitter and her assistant stepped inside the changing area; Melanie waited outside. They helped me get into the dress, which looked airy and pliable but was actually heavy and stiff underneath the arms. It didn't feel great, but it looked great. Like it was made for me. (Which it was.) Everything fit perfectly.

The outfitter secured a rope of pearls around my neck, while the assistant applied fat pearl studs to each of my six ear holes. Then they produced a sensational pair of Jimmy Chang heels, with UrSkin™ technology. I stepped in and instantly felt divine.

"Can I just say? You don't look sick at all. You look fabulous" the assistant said.

"Truly fabulous," the outfitter agreed.

"Thank you, ladies," I mumbled. I saw the girl in the mirror, standing tall and proud in her Y$800 pumps, wearing a dress that exposed little, but just enough to always remind you that this wasn't merely a person, this was a *woman*. And she didn't look like she was dying of Stage IV lung cancer, even with the whitening Goth makeup she'd applied to her normally rosy cheeks. And the more I stared at the girl in the mirror, the more I wanted to cry.

For a few seconds there, I really thought I wasn't going to be able to go through with it. I got stuck and scared.[51]

Then I reminded myself that "I" don't really exist, except as an intellectual concept, and that living or dying isn't going to change the amount of energy in the universe. The invisible molecules will get rearranged slightly. That's all. I'm not that important.

"Ready?" the outfitter said, smiling cheerfully and gesturing toward the door.

I made myself smile bravely. "The real answer is, 'I don't know,' but let's just say *yes.*"

"Well, that's great!" she said.

---

[51] Sort of like right now. I'm really scared you guys.

I was escorted down the hall to another room, a large room. It looked like a media studio, or a theater. Shiny floors, strong lights on tracks, cooled air. The kind of place where you would construct a multimedia event. One entire wall was covered floor2ceiling with a green scrim. People wearing headsets stood in the shadows.

"Wow. You look amazing." I turned to see Coach Mike, nodding enthusiastically at me. "Nice."

"Thanks. I think?" I replied. I was having second – and third and fourth – thoughts. Then I considered my fellow human beings, my brothers and sisters. I thought of them enslaved, reduced to beasts of burden for other human beings, and I got strong. "Let's do this thing, Coach Mike!"

"All right, then," he said, staring directly at my tits.

It was explained to me by my handlers that although they weren't at liberty to divulge the actual location of my mission – indeed, they themselves hadn't yet been notified from the higher-ups – they had been provided an outline of the next day's events. We would run our simulation based on the outline; however, they stressed, the actual mission could be different in many ways and so I needed to be ready to adjust quickly. Did I understand?

"I do," I said, feeling like this was the wedding I'll never have.

A tall man, maybe 40-something, emerged from the darkness at the edge of the room. He was wearing a military uniform, cut well and adorned with a mosaic of medals. He had exceptionally blue

249

eyes, exceptionally white teeth, and an exceptionally chiseled jaw. Super handsome, super male. "This is Colonel Flurk," Coach Mike said. "He'll be your mission controller. He's in charge."

"Ms. Galt," the Colonel said, staring in my eyes. "The pleasure is all mine." He extended his hand, the one without the wedding ring.

"Colonel Flurk," I said, staring back at him, placing my little hand in his. He squeezed gently, and then a little more firmly.

He had a flat, Midwestern voice, with like a three-note range. No emotion. "On behalf of the United States of America, I thank you, Ms. Galt, for your selfless service to the men and women of this great country. We are all grateful and humbled by your patriotism."

"We all do what we can, Colonel," I said, smiling my best I've-got-a-secret smile. "Some of us are just lucky to be able to do more than others."

"That's a fine attitude, ma'am," he said. "That's what heroes are made of."

My smile widened, because I really did have a secret. "Each of us has her own definition of 'hero,' Colonel Flurk. I wonder if you'll be telling people I'm a hero once I'm gone."

His eyes flashed with annoyance. "Of course I will," he said measuredly. "And so will other proud Americans. They'll be talking about you until the end of their days. And so will their children and grandchildren. You'll always be remembered as a great American hero."

"That's reassuring," I told him.

The Colonel nodded approvingly. "We admire your positive attitude and your sunny disposition." Everyone around us seemed to be nodding, too. "Great attitude."

People murmured their agreement and affirmation. Very supportive, these handlers.

"Now, ma'am, if you're ready?" Colonely Flurk said, gesturing toward the green screen. "We're going to begin your mission simulation."

"Ready," I said, trying maybe a bit too hard to sound ready. The truth was (and is) that I wasn't ready. I'm still not ready! You're *never* ready – not until the moment you can honestly say *there's nothing else I'd rather do with my life than die for a righteous cause.*

I can still think of a thing or two. Like, *if Jonah would contact me right now*...maybe it's not too late?

No, it's too late. Way too late. I know too much. It's been too late for a long time.

They guided me to a spot in front of the screen marked on the floor with a Termite Squad logo, instead of an X. Nice touch, I thought. Coach Mike stood on one side of me and the Colonel on the other. They spoke in hushed tones. "Ms. Galt," the Colonel said, "what you're about to experience will feel very real. If I didn't tell you in advance that it was all holographic, you would never guess. Our guys are good."

"The best," Coach Mike added.

"Right. And because of the elevated veracity levels you'll be working with, I want to emphasize that you might be confused, you might forget that this is all happening right here, not at the actual site of your mission." Colonel Flurk smiled. "Amazing what they can do with these things," he said, looking approvingly at the green scrim.

When I leaned in and peered closely at the fabric, I could see billions of not-quite-invisible silver filaments woven into endless grids.

There was a hissing sound, like steam escaping a teapot. I turned to see the entire studio enveloped by more green scrims extending from the floor to the ceiling. They billowed outward, spreading around the room, until it seemed that every perpendicular surface was shrouded.

"Immersive technology is the term," Coach Mike reported. "Developed by the Air Force."

Flurk nodded approvingly. "State of the art. Only a few civilians have ever seen this."

I said, "I'm honored."

"Yes. So are we. Honored to train you."

I didn't know what to say, so I said, "Thank you." Coach Mike nodded and returned his gaze to my décolletage.

Suddenly an upper corner of the studio began to glow blue, and I could see a glassed-in booth, with people in it. "Control center," Flurk explained. "You won't see it once the simulation begins."

"Can I look inside?" I asked, genuinely curious about what all these people with headsets actually did.

"Negative. No. That's not possible."

I shrugged. "OK. Whatever." Deep down I was a little surprised. I thought dying girls got everything they asked for.

Flurk seemed to stand straighter. "Ms. Galt? Shall we?"

Before I could answer, the room went dark. All I could see was the control booth, glowing reassuringly, shimmering with the unmistakable light of plasmatic monitors and next-generation Armscreens.® A disembodied male voice whispered in my ear, "Good morning, Ms. Galt. I'm Dylan, your lead Communicator. I'll be with you today and tomorrow at all times."

"I can hear you," I said into the near-dark. "Can you hear me?"

"Oh, yes. Your algo-chip has been properly calibrated to sync with the broadcaster sewn into your dress." I touched the hemline, where it felt stiff. "Um, actually, it's closer to your neckline." Apparently, Dylan had no trouble seeing me. "By the way, you look really great."

Flustered, I didn't immediately respond.

"Ms. Galt? Joan?"

"Yes. I'm here. I can hear you."

"Ah, good." Dylan had a remarkably calming voice, gentle like Portuguese cotton. I thought I could also make out Flurk's voice in the background, intoning orders to his team. "So, right. Yes. Good. We're in full communication and ready to proceed."[52]

For a second, nothing happened. I thought maybe our link had been broken. Then, like magic, my bed appeared beside me – my bed from home, my actual bed, with the duvet and pillowcases I like. It didn't slowly take form; it was just there, *snap*, just like that.

Dylan in my ear: "Termite Joan, get in your bed."

It looked so real, so three-dimensional. Could this really be a holograph? No. I touched my bed. It was solid. It was a thing. It was furniture.

"Is this my actual bed?" I asked.

Flurk in my ear: "Termite Joan, we can't interrupt the simulation with further questions."

Dylan: "Get in your bed, please, Termite Joan."

I put both hands on the quilt, hiked a knee up, and rolled myself onto the mattress. It felt exactly like my mattress feels like.[53]

"Get under the covers," Dylan instructed, his voice firm but unthreatening.

I began to peel back the blankets – the same white one and red one I've used for years. The ones Jonah and I picked out together. With prodding from Flurk, who I could hear vaguely through my Communicator's microphone, Dylan told me that

---

[52] No idea what my Communicator looks like. Never saw his face. He sounded kind.

[53] I'm lying on it as I input this. The similarity is/was uncanny.

during the actual mission I wouldn't wear my dress and pearls to bed. "Just whatever you usually wear."

"Nothing?" I proposed.

"Sure." I swear I could hear leering noises in the background.

I got underneath the covers. The linens smelled like me. The pillow wasn't similar to my pillow, it *was* my pillow. At least it seemed that way.

Dylan cooed, "Good night, Termite Joan. We'll see you in the morning, for your mission." Before I could respond, the room got even darker. The blue glow faded to black. The hum of energy and activity went quiet. It was night.

It must have been around 11AM, but I would have sworn to you that it was the middle of the night and I was snuggled in the comfort of my home cocoon. Not too warm, not too cold, the perfect balance of soft fabric and strong back support. Comforting. Delicious... Peaceful...I felt myself becoming sleepy. I felt my breath slow. I started to see images on the back of my eyelids, and I understand now, in hindsight, that I was totally asleep, right there in the training studio.

I think I was dreaming, although it's possible they were able to simulate that, too.

I'm in a meadow, with wildflowers taller than me, obscuring the horizon. The sky above is a brilliant, non-plasmatic blue. I'm swimming now, treading my way through the wildflowers, swimming through red and yellow and orange and pink – and it's just so vibrant!

Yes. Yes, I can feel vibrations, pleasant tingling tremors on my breasts and the small of my back. I'm being massaged by a group of sunflowers. They're bent over me, brushing gently against me, petting me. I hear myself moan.

They stand at attention, and their faces become satellite dishes pointed to the sky, which suddenly has grown dark and forbidding.

Now it's raining.

The raindrops are jellybeans. They don't hurt me as they fall to earth. I open my mouth and they slowly settle on my tongue. Just the right amount. Delicious, chewy. Fruity.

Before I can swallow, it's Jonah's tongue in my mouth. We're in my bed. Our bed. We're kissing. We're making love. He's going down on me.

Then it's a gorgeous Ethiopian woman from my college days, a girl I always liked but never hooked with. God, she's good! I reach for her head between my thighs and I find Marcy's boyish hair. I pull her up, towards my belly and chest and finally my mouth.

Just as our lips are about to meet, an awful buzzing fills my head. Marcy disappears. The noise gets louder.

It's my alarm. It's going off.

I'm awake.

I'm in my bedroom at home. Awake.

I rub my Armscreen® to snooze. A few more delicious minutes…But the alarm comes back immediately, and now I'm really awake.

256

Yes, I'm in my bedroom. There's my dresser. There's the photo of me and Jonah on the nightstand. In the corner of the room, near the door, the charging station.

My arm says it's 08:30 on December 31, 2090. I think, You sure slept late! *Then I feel the unfamiliar pressure of a necklace, and I realize I'm wearing my customized Endvest™. It's that day.*

My "Thought of the Day" appears before feeds commence: "Having an open mind is a sign of intelligence; having a closed mind is the opposite. Therefore, stubbornness is an undesirable trait and 'willingness to change' is a desirable one."

Before I can ponder that one, an Urgent Alert flashes and buzzes on my arm: **In 30 minutes you will have visitors. Use the toilet, review your Mission Outline, and recheck your travel kit containing only pre-authorized items. TY.**

I do as instructed, although it's hard to go when you start to suspect they can see and hear you. Lifting my dress and pulling down my thong isn't easy in this thing. Everything's stiff.

I go to the kitchen. A disposable monitor (which I know isn't mine, since I don't purchase anything disposable, not even cheap stuff like razor blades and monitors), glows from the middle of the table. It's my Mission Outline.

I think, OK, my Mission Outline is on the table. My father's broken *accumulation* is hanging on the wall. This all seems to be really happening.

The safety seal on the monitor is cracked, indicating I've read this before, which is odd,

*because I have no memory of ever seeing my
Mission Outline before this moment. When I review
it, the similarities to Tiffany Amber Liu's are
obvious. I quickly determine that it's basically the
same plan as hers, with some of the times changed.*

*I scroll through, looking for details, for hints
on my destination...none. It's boilerplate I've
already read dozens of times. I already know how
this is going to go, and how it will end.*

*For a moment, I start to question the whole
Termite Squad concept. I wonder for a second if
100-year-olds are mentally and physically
competent enough to be heroes. But I quickly
suppress the thought. I have the weird feeling they
can hear what I'm thinking – and that they just
heard me think that!*

*So I just stop thinking, as much as I can. It's
really not too hard to do.*

*I don't think about Jonah. I don't think
about my Dads. About my life. Nothing. I just sit
there, meditating on the white light, starting to feel
peaceful and calm.*

*From the most distant edge of my
perception, a voice, my voice, creeps into my
consciousness. It says,* Have you considered the
possibility that they're making you not think?
Because that's what they want?

*Then I wonder how I could have such a
thought if they're really in control...and I go back
to being the master of my thoughtlessness.
Ommmmmmmmmmmmmmmmmm.*

*At precisely 09:00 my locked front door
swings open and in walk three men wearing white
exterminator uniforms. I immediately recognize
Coach Mike. The other two, vaguely. "Good
morning, Ms. Galt!" Coach Mike says to me, with
what I take to be way too much cheerfulness.*

"Good morning, Coach Mike."

"We're here for your termite problem."

*I guess they're not controlling everything I
think, because I think (but don't say):* My building
is made entirely of steel and glass.

*What I say is, "Good. I've been waiting for
you." By now I've figured out that the other two
guys, tall and broad, are Termite Valets, and I half
expect them to produce a wheelchair for me.*

*Coach Mike motions for me to follow him. I
stand. He turns to go. I can see the back of his
uniform. It says* Termite Squad, *with the logo.*

*The TVs flank me as we walk out the door.
At the time, I don't have any pangs of realization
that I'll never see my home again. I step out into the
hallway of my unit, like it's just another day at the
office.*[54]

*Somehow I have the presence of mind to
realize this is all being simulated – that's my gut
feeling when my neighbors emerge from their units,
applauding for me as I pass, as though I were
Zingpin Li, or Molly Pradhash, someone who makes
people gasp. The adulation is overwhelming. My*

---

[54] Now I'm suspicious about why I didn't feel
anything.

*heart feels fluttery. I clutch at my chest – and I
realize I'm not wearing the pearl necklace...and,
OMG, I'm not wearing the little black dress!*

I'm having a naked dream, that's what it is.

*Wait, I'm not. I feel myself. I'm wearing my
favorite gray flannel fair-trade sweatshirt and my
favorite American-made stretchies. I don't know
why or how, but I feel good. I feel comfortable.
Calm.*

*The TVs guide me to the emergency stairs,
at the end of the hallway. Just before they open the
door, I think I catch a glimpse of Flurk's control
booth, glowing over the "Exit" sign.*

*Then I think I see Marcy, clapping for me,
standing with my neighbors, none of whom I fully
recognize, all of whom look vaguely familiar.*

*Then, just before I pass through the
doorway's threshold, I think I see Jonah standing
next to Marcy. I want to cry out, but the image
disappears instantly.*

*Coach Mike, the TVs and I are standing on
the landing, about to walk down the stairs. Coach
Mike shakes and cocks his head. The TVs grasp me
gently by each arm. "Up," Coach Mike says. "To
the roof."*

*I ask no questions. I climb the stairs. Two
flights. "Your physical fitness is greatly
appreciated," Coach Mike says, warmly. I nod in
reply, seemingly dumbstruck.*

*We arrive at the roof. When one of the TVs
opens the door, it's suddenly loud and bright, an
assault of sound and light. I can't see anything, and*

I shield my eyes with my hands. I hear Coach Mike order, "Now!"

I feel a soft bag being slipped over my head. It's immediately quieter and darker. Much more pleasant. I can see enough to make out large shapes, but that's about it. The roaring seems to have ceased, and I can hear perfectly – probably because there's audio technology sewn in the fabric. Dylan the Communicator is in my ear: "Good morning, Termite Joan...you can reply."

"Good morning."

"You've been inoculated from certain sights and sounds for your own protection. The safety helmet you're wearing will remain on your head until you arrive at your destination. This is for your own protection. Now, sit back and relax."

I feel the TVs guiding me into a seated position, and then reclining. I sense that I'm on a gurney, and I'm being wheeled. After some gentle jostling, the movement stops. I hear doors closing and motors humming, and then the feeling of being lifted, as though the gurney I'm lying on is hydraulic.

No, that's not it. I can tell now: I'm flying. We're flying. A helicopter? An F-44, with rotating jet packs? I don't know, and it seems unimportant to ask.

Dylan in my ear: "Termite Joan, you'll be arriving very soon."

A minute later – less? – I can feel a different sort of pressure on my back. We seem to be descending. It gets very loud for a few seconds, and then nothing. I can make out the familiar voice of Coach Mike. "OK. We're here." I can't tell if we've traveled 8,000 miles or eight. My perception of time and distance has disappeared.

Dylan in my ear: "Termite Joan, you can remain relaxed. Your valets will take care of everything...you can reply."

"I understand."

More gentle jostling, more latches. And now I'm moving again, being wheeled. Only in retrospect do I realize that I never wonder where we're going. I seem to understand that it doesn't matter. We'll get there when we get there, and when we do, I'll follow my training.

Dylan in my ear: "Termite Joan, you'll be arriving very soon."

I feel the gurney being reconfigured into a chair. I feel the TVs' hands on me, careful and respectful. The inside of the hood gradually goes from dark to light, to an approximation of daylight. Now, the hood comes off – and it's daylight, and I'm sitting in what looks like a very nice hotel suite (I can see a very big bed and other standard furnishings) with Coach Mike and the two TVs. Behind them, a giant wallscreen. The curtains are drawn in front of the windows, but I can sense that the sun is still out. I have an impulse to stand and look out the window, but before I do, the wallscreen begins to glow and an Urgent Alert appears: **Walk into the bathroom...You will be met there.**

I check my arm to see if the message has been repeated there. My Armscreen® is missing. It's gone.

Dylan in my ear: "For your own protection."

I stand. I feel normal. Rested. Balanced.

Content.

Dylan: "You've been fully disconnected."

I know I can reply, but I don't want to. I'm enjoying this new feeling. Involuntarily – instinctively? – I keep glimpsing at my arm, doing the familiar thumb-twist, exposing the crook of my elbow. Skin and veins are where my screen is supposed to be. Eventually I stop looking at my arm and start touching it instead. The area just below my wrist is remarkably sensitive, pleasurably so. I feel as though I've discovered a new erogenous zone – which makes me smirk. Now? *Now's when I find out how sweet life can be? #sickhumor*

I laugh, because I know if I don't I'm going to cry, and if I do I might not be able to...No. No, no, that's weak thinking. I'm not going there. I'm OK. I don't need to cry and I don't need to laugh. I need to serve.

I stride into the bathroom. Melanie the Outfitter is in there, with a female assistant dressed like one of the TVs. It's roomy.

"The bathtub has been removed for your mission," Dylan explains in my ear.

I stop myself from thinking that he knows what I'm thinking. I do that by putting my attention off of myself and my thoughts, which, after all, I'm supposed to be in control of – they don't control me! – and I refocus my attention on the little black dress that Melanie is holding, like she's an OIP Showroom Model.

"Stunning," I say. "To die for." No one laughs.

"Termite Joan, your dress," Melanie says, handing me the chic evening frock that I've already started thinking of as "my little black dress," as if it's my go-to choice for a night on the town. It really is fabulous.

I take it from her. She motions toward a screened –off changing area, where I presume the tub was situated previous to sacrificing itself for Termite Squad service. I step behind the screen, which the assistant closes behind me.

I start to remove my sweatshirt. "Dylan? Mission Control?"

I hear Dylan clear his throat. "Yes?"

"Can you see me right now?"

"You mean…"

"Can you see me changing?"

"You're in full view. Yes. For your own protection."

"OK." I remove my clothes, telling myself I'm doing a good thing. For my community. For my sisters and brothers. I don't let myself think about the eyes on my naked skin. I can't. I have a mission to accomplish.

Quickly down to my thong and bra, my favorite ones, the most comfy, I slip into my little black dress. It feels against my body exactly as it

*did when I first tried it on -- which seems like it was
only seconds ago…it feels perfect. Another layer of
skin, but even softer. I know I must look sensational
because I* feel *sensational.*

*I step out. Melanie and her assistant make
gaspy faces. "Oh, my," they say, clutching their
chests.*

*"Here," Melanie says, putting the pearls
around my neck while the assistant fills my ear
holes. "Let's get you properly accessorized." It
doesn't take long. I step into the Jimmy Changs
placed before my feet, and I'm finished.*

*Melanie gives me the once over. She nods.
"Go look," she says.*

*There I am, in the mirror: It's me, Joan
Galt. But somehow I've been transformed into a
Media star, maybe even an Avatar! I'm wearing the
dress, and now my hair's been done, and I'm
wearing makeup, artfully applied. I look like I'm
ready to accept an award. Or present one. I smile at
myself.* Hello, good looking. *And then I smile even
more, because I know I'm such a goof.*

*Dylan in my ear: "You're happy and
content, Termite Joan?"*

"Yes," I answer. And it's the truth.

*"Good," he says. His voice really is quite
nice. Soothing. "We think you deserve that feeling."*

I start to think, Yes, we all do, yet so few of
us…. *But I stop myself. Distribution problems
should not be my mental focus right now…I must
simply accept being happy and content and not*

worry about the unhappiness and discontent of others.

The Termite Valets appear at my side. Dylan says, "You'll have some time now for a brief rest before your big night."

"We're not going now?" I say.

"No, Termite Joan. We'll tell you when you're going...Until then, you'll have some time for a brief rest...you can reply."

"I understand."

The TVs escort me to a handsome upholstered chair, probably an antique from the 20th Century. It looks like something my mother would have had in the family's summer place, out near the reclaimed Montauk ruins. The one I was never invited to. It's a lovely chair, puffy, welcoming. They guide me to sit in it. As I lean back, I feel the protective hood being slipped over my head.

Dylan in my ear: "This will help you rest."

Everything is quiet and dark. I feel the chair transforming into a recliner. I'm on a bed, it feels like. I'm on my own bed, it feels like. Yes. Yes, now I'm in my bed, at home. I'm on my pillow. I reach over to Jonah's spot and feel the blankets, our blankets. He's not there, but it smells like him. I inhale deeply, taking him in my nostrils. I really do feel so peaceful and happy and content. I could just sleep forever.

That's the last thing I remember: I'm in my bed at home and I fall asleep. No dreams. No awareness of time and space. Gone.

The Termite Squad:
My Official and Authentic Report

When I'm awakened by the gentle prodding of the Termite Valets, their hands sheathed in white gloves, it seems like it's only a minute later. But the hood is off my head, and I'm sitting up in the chair, there in the middle of the hotel suite. I can sense somehow that it's night-time, that many hours have passed. I'm wearing my little black dress.

"Good evening, Termite Joan." It's the comforting sound of Dylan the Communicator in my ear. "We hope you rested well."

"I don't remember anything."

"Excellent. And we hope you rested well."

"Oh, yes. I did."

"Good. We'll need your full attention now, Termite Joan. Things are going to start moving quickly."

"I understand."

"But first," Dylan says, "please use the facilities. We've set aside five minutes for that."

"OK," I say, nodding. Can they see me? I'm sure they can, so I don't ask and I don't think about it. I just go. (Pee). I haven't eaten in like 12 hours, but I'm not hungry in the slightest. Or thirsty. I just feel really good. Even peeing for them on their cameras, I feel good.

I consider for a second that this could be my last pee, ever. But somehow the thought comes and goes before I can fixate on it. Instead, I seem to be able to acknowledge the facts – the truth – dispassionately, as though I'm a step removed from the proceedings. Yes, that might have been the last

*time I'll urinate here on this troubled planet. And
yes, I'm flushing. And yes, also, my clothes fit so
nicely, even with the Endvest™ sewn into the silk
lining.*

It's all good.

*There's the magic switch, welded or glued
or something inside the hemline. When seated, the
switch rests between my thighs, just in front of my
thong-covered* katori. *I finger it. (The switch). Feels
just like the one I practiced on. Two hands. Up-and-
to-the-right.*

*Dylan in my ear: "Termite Joan, please
refrain from touching the switch until instructed."*

I nod.

"Thanks for your understanding."

*I look in the mirror – and I can feel the
physical sensation of my nascent narcissism
intensifying. I can literally feel pride swelling in my
chest, a tactile rush of tender tickling across my
front. I don't know why this is happening...but I
can't stop staring at myself. I look so good. Like, I
want to look away but I can't. This isn't how I
normally feel when I see myself in the mirror.*

*I don't look like I'm dying of cancer. I look
amazing. "Are you doing this to me?" I hear myself
say out loud.*

"Please repeat that, Termite Joan."

*But I've already figured out that they are
doing this to me, making me fall in love with my
visage, so I silently shake off the thought – no, no-
no-no – and just serenely accept my new levels of*

*beauty. When I turn to gaze once more at my
plummy cheeks and pimped-out lips, glistening like
they've just made a girl come, Joan Galt is no
longer in the mirror.*

It's Jonah.

*It's a version of him. It's me as him. A
hybrid.*

*I can feel all my biometrics spinning out of
control. I'm losing the good feeling. I'm panicking.
This isn't right.*

*I'm sure they can tell. I'm sure – did they do
this?...No. They –*

*"Termite Joan, everything is great," Dylan
coos in his gentlest tones. I'm in love with his voice.
"We already know about your brother. Your half-
brother, I should say."*

*Yes, of course, they do. And I can feel it,
right in the same place where I could feel the pride
swelling, I can feel it right there: they want me to
feel ashamed. They want shame to replace my
abundant self-love.*

And I'm not sure I can stop them.

*I feel the words slipping out of my mouth,
and I hear them being pronounced in my voice. But
I'm a spectator to all this. A bystander. "Having
sexual relations with my brother Jonah was a
terrible tragedy that did lasting damage to my
psyche. Indeed, our incestuous relationship might,
in fact, be the source of my terminal lung cancer,
the way I'm punishing my body."*

269

*Dylan in my ear: "You are loved, Termite
Joan. You are appreciated. Your country considers
you a hero."*

*"Thank you," I say, genuinely grateful for
his kindness.*

*"Whatever happened before tonight isn't
going to matter. Only your service will matter."[55]*

"Right."

*"Good. So. We shall proceed." Dylan
sounds very relaxed, but also a little excited. "Look
in the mirror," he says.*

*Jonah's gone. It's me. Joan Galt. Beautiful,
confident, prepared. A modern American Hero.*

I say, "Let's do this thing."

*And when I do, everything fades once more
to a comforting black. I'm in my protective hood
again, and I sense I've been positioned to lie down.
I see a distant white light, glowing with a purple
penumbra, far away in a distant region of the
endless screen stretching boundlessly before my
third eye. It seems to be coming toward me, slowly
and steadily, getting perceptibly larger as it nears
the center of my mind's universe. I follow the light
and I hear nothing, not even my own breath.*

---

[55] It's occurred to me that this sounds good, but it's
not really true. I mean, people are still arguing
about Tiffany Amber Liu's personal life, not
celebrating her heroism. I'm sure the same thing
will happen to me.

Faintly, barely audible, I hear Dylan's voice in my ear and in my chest and in my belly and everywhere: "Termite Joan, you've arrived."

The white light retreats and disappears. My screen goes gray and then white – and then I can see.

I see I'm in the passenger section of a Teslarian transporter, the big kind they use for bachelorette parties. I'm wearing my little black dress, and the pearls. The TVs – my *Termite Valets, I think of them – are here…and so is someone else, someone I've never seen before.*

An old woman. A very old woman. A Centurion, I would guess. She's sitting in a wheeled chair, parked against the wall of the transporter, with another uniformed Valet beside her.

"That's Candace," Dylan explains in my ear. "A fellow Termite."

I look at her, trying to make eye contact. "Don't attempt to engage her in conversation," Dylan instructs. "She's not really capable of that."

Candace's face is a giant rictus of sadness, with an epic frown bisecting her head. She stares at the floor, half asleep. Her hands are folded in her lap, on top of a quilted blanket. And I can see poking through her fingers the magic switch.

My fingers go directly to my *magic switch, at the hemline. Yes, it's there. I let it go and discourage myself from playing with it.*

"Soon," Dylan assures me.

The Termite Squad:
My Official and Authentic Report

The transporter's exit door opens. I can sense it's nighttime, wherever we are. How long I've been supine, how long we've been traveling – that's all unknowable and irrelevant. We've arrived. We're moving.

One of my TVs helps his colleague wheel Candace out of the transporter and onto what looks like some kind of loading dock or delivery bay. The other TV motions for me to follow. I step into the night air. It's more than chilly. It's bitterly cold against my bare arms. It stings. I've long since stopped wondering if this is real. It's terribly awfully real.

We're whisked behind a heavy steel door, and the coldness is instantly replaced by the comforting warmth of solar circulators and heated stone floorpieces. "No more discomfort," Dylan purrs in my ear. "You're going to feel perfect. All your pains will vanish soon. You'll be free."

How glorious those words sound, like I'm getting a massage. "All living creatures shall be free," I hear myself saying. Candace looks very sad to me. I want her to be free from her sadness.

"That's fine, Termite Joan."

When I turn away from Candace, I see that my TV has changed into formal wear and a bowtie. He looks very handsome. I glance back at Candace, and now her TV is all dressed nice, too. Candace looks the same: hunched, bedraggled, radiating misery.

I remind myself to stand up straight.

The Termite Squad:
My Official and Authentic Report

Candace and her chaperone leave through another door. It seems very quiet, wherever we are.

My handsome TV offers his arm. I take it. We leave through the same door as Candace, but she's vanished.

Now we're standing in a vast, silent room, with a towering ceiling, so high I have to tilt my head back yogi-like to see the top. It's very dark, but I can make out large shapes suspended from the ceiling – arty objects, I imagine. Or massive chandeliers. My eyes are still adjusting to the murk.

The floor, which clicks against my heels, reflects what little light gets into this cavernous space. I can see enough to know that Candace and her TV aren't here.

Dylan in my ear: "Her mission is elsewhere."

"I should have said goodbye," I announce.

"You did," Dylan assures me.

"Oh, good," I say, unconcerned about what I can no longer remember.

"Now, it's all about you. It's Termite time." He sounds very encouraging. I'm really not the least bit frightened anymore. I'm curious and eager, the way you feel when you're scheduled for a first date OIP and you just know it's going to go well. Very positive and up.

"Your 'metrics are great, Termite Joan," Dylan reports. He seems to be looking over a series of read-outs. "Your contentment numbers are truly lofty."

I feel an impulse to check my arm, but it passes immediately. "That's so great!" I reply, feeling utterly carefree, as though there were no past and no future, feeling like I'm connected to an eternal Present.

My TV has become even more handsome, slightly taller and broader. Strong. I like the way he looks at me, approvingly and with an obvious hunger that announces itself no matter how strenuously he tries to hide it. "This is fun," I announce.

He smiles at me warmly. I feel beautiful.

We walk slowly, arm in arm. No chatting. No awkwardness. Just an abiding satisfaction in the silence, interrupted only by the rhythmic clacking of our shoes on the floor. I don't know where we are, and I don't care. It really is all good. It really is!

My eyes adjust to the gloom, and I can see now that the massive forms hanging from the ceiling are animals – stuffed and preserved animals, hanging from wires, as though they were still flying and swimming through space, unbothered by gravity. I can make out a giant tail shape, and as I walk nearer I see that it's a whale! A whole whale floating in the air. It's magical. It's delightful. It makes me smile. I don't know why.

My handsome TV smiles, too, and we keep walking, synchronized perfectly, neither leading nor following. I realize then that I'm holding in my free hand a small purse, a stylish little black and silver clutch.

Dylan in my ear: "You can open it."

The Termite Squad:
My Official and Authentic Report

I stop walking. My TV stands beside me and allows me to withdraw my arm from his. I open the purse. In the near-dark, I can sense there are three objects inside: Cloropellets™, a lip coloring moisturizer pen, and a single condom in a foil wrapper.

I finger the rubber and turn bashfully to my Valet. He's looking at the floor.

"You can open it," Dylan says.

"Now?"

"Yes."

This seems like a weird spot, but I'm not deterred. I tear open the packet, wondering what highly imaginative scenario they've devised for me and Mr. Gorgeous. Inside, there's a ring of metal with a circumference of an erect penis. It fits around my three middle fingers scrunched together. It doesn't feel like it would be comfortable on a man.

"Place the ring around your Termite switch," Dylan tells me. I reach down and find it beneath my dress. The ring slips right over it, just like a condom is supposed to when you've got it right-side-up. I can feel the ring snap into place, flush against the interior fabric of my Endvest™.

"A final safety precaution," Dylan explains. "You've been authenticated, secured, and engaged. Nothing bad can happen now. No accidents. Only the plan."

"Oh, that's marvelous," I reply, because it really is marvelous how everything eventually works out for the best, as though there's a Master

Plan and there's someone smart and able enough to execute it.

Needing no instruction now, fully aware of how to proceed to the next moment after this one, I take my TV's arm, bow my head demurely, and walk leisurely with him down the hallway, toward a faint sound that seems to be emanating from very far away, more a low vibrational rumble than a distinct sound. But I can feel it. I know my escort can, too. We're very connected. Him, me, all the animals in the air, all the people I've met and all the people I'll never meet. We're all connected.

It's a great feeling, this sense of belonging to something so much larger and grander than you could previously grasp. It's like I've just made love and I'm drifting off to dreams, spent with pleasure, but fully awake in my sleep. Each step is a mini orgasm, each breath a soft shudder of joy running through my sternum. I'm knowing bliss. What awaits me at the end of the hallway doesn't yet exist, and either does my life before I opened my purse. It's all right now, beginning and ending inside the center of my mind.

With serenity comes light. Is the sun rising, or have my pupils dilated to new widths? I don't care – I can see.

I see dinosaurs! I see dinosaurs with wings, and with ferocious teeth! I see them raised up on hind legs, emitting terrible silent roars. I see dinosaurs grazing on slender wisps of savannah grass. I see big ones chasing little ones running for their life.

*I'm not afraid. All these dinosaurs are
frozen, paralyzed, like plaster casts at a museum.
From certain angles, I can discern what seems like
reflected light pulsing from the area around some of
these creatures...a few spectacular steps closer,
feeling better and freer and altogether more well
with each footfall, I see that some of the dinosaurs
are indeed encased in a glass-like box, transparent
but solid, -- again, like display cases at a museum.*

*Beside our path, standing sentry, I find a
tree stump, high as my waist. Other stumps line the
way. I feel the one closest to me. It's smooth and
polished – but not flat. I can make out some raised
bumps on the surface. My fingers rest on one of
these bumps, rounded and soft against my palm. I
feel the urge to press against it with my hand. The
bump gives way slightly, and then I hear Dylan's
honey voice in my ear. "Following the Jurassic
period, scientists speculate that a dramatic change
in climate, brought about by meteor strikes, caused
mass extinctions of Earth's dominant species."*

*My handsome Valet leads me down the
hallway. He seems to know where we are and where
we're going.*

"From a new group of competitive species,
homo sapiens, *the Human, rose to the top of the
food chain." Dylan sounds like a tour guide in my
ear.*

*Now I see cavemen wearing hides and
covered in hair. They're crouched around the
orange embers of a warming fire. Apelike, with
prognathous jaws and long arms and big feet, they
look like wild animals. An involuntary jolt of fear
passes through me. I can feel my heart quicken.*

*"You're in no danger, Termite Joan," Dylan
says, in a tone that suggests unalarmed concern. He
genuinely cares about my well-being. "You're
safe."*

"Am I...?

*"You know where you are," Dylan
reassures me. "You know."*

*Yes. I do. I know now I'm not stranded in the
past, a time-jumping victim of bad physics. I know
I'm not inside my head, either. I know I'm in the
present. I know this is happening. And I know where
I am.*

*"I'm in a museum," I say out loud, and the
chills that run through my nipples and the back of
my knees are like electricity. I know where I am!
I'm in a museum. I've been here before!* This
museum.

"Yes," Dylan reassures me. "Yes you are."

*Yes, I am. I can see clearly now. My eyes
have adjusted to the gloom. I'm not just in any
museum.*

I'm in the Smithsonian.

*"I used to come here with my dads," I
announce to no one. No one answers. Maybe I'm
imagining all of this.*

*"You're not imagining this," Dylan says,
with a little chuckle in his voice.*

*No, I'm not. This is real. I know exactly
where I am! Now I can see familiar exhibits
demonstrating "Darwin's Theory of Evolution" and
"Man's Impact on the Environment," which was*

*famously removed and put into storage for nearly
20 years, in the dark times prior to the 2nd Civil
War. (My dads took me when it was re-installed –
right around the same time that they got their jobs
back.) I see directional signs leading to the insect
area, and the ocean creatures section. And to the
exit.*

*My handsome Termite Valet seems to be
leading me there, towards the exit. I don't
understand what's happening, but I don't have any
motivation or impulse to ask. I'm following, quite
happily.*

*We come to an intersection of hallways,
near the spot where Mammals and Birds blend
together. To the left, far away, maybe at the very
end of the hallway, which seems at least a city block
away, I can make out clearly a few concentrated
beams of light leaking into the distant blackness, the
kind of light that comes from beneath doors and
through cracks between curtains.*

*I can also hear very faintly a pulsing
vibration of energy, no louder than a heartbeat in a
frightened girl's head, but definitely audible.*

*We walk toward the light, toward the sound.
This hallway is darker than the first one, and
whatever is on exhibit in the display cases lining the
hallway – more stuffed animals, I would imagine --
remains obscured by the dark. I must have walked
down this very hallway at some point in my
childhood, even if I can't say for certain which
branch of the Smithsonian I'm currently traversing.
There's something familiar and unthreatening here.
I'm not afraid. Not at all. I can sense the stilled life*

all around me, immobile yet present. All the creatures are with me.

So serene do I feel that it doesn't occur to me to wonder why I'm here, literally within bicycling distance of my home, instead of, say, Venezuela or Pakistan, some harsh and lonely place far from everything that's familiar and comforting. It doesn't occur to me at this moment that I'll be the first Termite Hero to complete her service on domestic soil. No, at this moment I'm not thinking about anything, except what's at the end of the hallway.

Every step brings the distant light closer, making it incrementally bigger and brighter, with each stride connecting to a master dimmer slider connected by telepathy to the beat of my locomotion. I'm controlling the light. My intention, my will to walk into the light, is what's making it grow.

Yes, it's true: I walk a little faster, and we're a little closer and the light is a little brighter. I am *the light!*

And the sound. I'm also the sound. It grows progressively louder and clearer with each successive footfall. Now I'm close enough to really hear: It's music.

*Music! All the vibrations of the universe arranged in a state of blissful harmony. It's down there. Yes. Yes, the sound, I can discern now, has a distinct rhythm...*ump-UMP-ump-UMP *– a pulse that matches the tempo of my feet. One, two, three, four. It feels good. 1-2-3-4. When did I learn this* *pleasure? Was I born with an understanding and a love for 1-2-3-4,* ump-Ump-ump-Ump? *I like it!*

I didn't know that sound and light could make me so happy.

Dylan in my ear: "How are you, Termite Joan?"

I giggle, feeling almost drunk with good feelings toward all living creatures, especially my Communicator with that glorious voice that flows through me like nectar, a warm river of calm that flows from my cilia into my veins, infusing me with peace. "You know how I feel," I say, teasingly. "Fabulous."

"That's marvelous, Termite Joan."

"Yes," I say, on the verge of a laughing attack. The light is nearer and the sound is slightly louder, and I can feel I'm really getting to where I'm meant to be going. Everything is going to be perfect.

The nearer I get, the better I feel. And I feel amazing. I feel pre-orgasmic, and the sensation intensifies by the second, with each forward motion. I want to walk faster, to get there. To come with pleasure! But every impulse to speed up is matched by an impulse to make it last, to prolong the ecstasy forever. I settle into what feels like the optimal pace. Soon, I'm in a kind of nirvana, the feeling you get with only the very best tantric sessions. But I'm having it all on my feet, standing up, walking to my ultimate destiny.

I know that they know I know they know that I know they're somehow making me feel this way. And but yet nonetheless I don't care.

"I'm happy," I think silently. And I imagine I hear Dylan in my ear saying, "That's good, Termite Joan." And I smile.

I smile, and I smile wider, and then time slows down and speeds up, and I'm drowning in pleasure and laughter, and I want to scream with joy, and I'm tingling, and almost moaning with every exhale, and feeling just perfect.

And then we're there. We're at the light, beside the sound.

I can see now that my Termite Valet and I are standing behind an immense heavy black curtain, a temporary wall, and the light I glimpsed from so far away, from the land of stuffed penguins, was actually seeping out through tiny cracks where the fabric doesn't quite completely touch the floor. The sound, I hear now, is in fact what I suspected: music. For sure. The old-fashioned real kind, with antique instruments from the 20th Century, played by real people. It's obvious. It sounds so quaint compared to bot-produced tracks. But older people like it, and I've got to admit it has a soothing effect, like Dylan's voice, a natural calmness about it that makes me feel utterly liberated from whatever anxieties I might have once had.

A woman is singing. Her voice is deep, rich, smoky. Another time. She's beckoning me with her sultry tones.

Let's take a trip to the promised land
You're not alone, I'll hold your hand

My TV motions toward a crack of light on the far side to his left. I follow him, It's only a few steps, and they're nice feeling ones, tiny tickles. When we arrive, standing beside the light beam, he gently removes his arm from mind, assumes the Namaste *pose with his hands and head, and speaks for the first and only time: "My mission is now complete. Yours continues. It's been an honor to serve beside you. Thank you, and farewell."*

And before I can say anything, he springs into the dark and walks away briskly, and then quickly, and now I can hear him running, sprinting into the blackness at the other end of the hallway. I'm alone.

But I'm not alone. I don't feel alone. I feel…

…There's someone waiting for me, there on the other side of the curtain. I can sense it. I can smell it. I know like a dog knows.

Yes. I know what to do. Dylan doesn't even have to tell me. I know: Walk into the light. Go. Walk into the light and sound.

Yes. Do it.

I do it.

The beam widens, accommodating my width. I'm blinded for a second by sheer whiteness. And then I can see again.

I'm in the Great Hall of the Smithsonian, with my back to the curtain. The crack is gone. I've passed over.

I'm standing in a solitary corner of the expansive room, obscured by potted palms and utility tarps cordoning off waste-bins and service materials. It seems like I'm standing in a temporary sanitation removal area, but it's totally clean.

Up high, stuffed creatures fill the airspace. The floor space has been cleared of dinosaurs and learning modules to make way for tables and chairs, and a large dance floor. The floor seems to be made of real wood, upon which hundreds of immaculately dressed people are clinched together doing an ancient dance fad called "the foxtrot." They're old people. Older people. Forties and up. They're wearing fancy dresses and kilts and saris, with fashionably accessorized Armscreens™ and the best shoes money can buy. Some of them, a few of them, are smiling and laughing.

It's a party. I'm at a party. And dressed appropriately. Nice! I don't have to try to smile. I'm smiling.

Dylan in my ear: "Termite Joan, walk to your right and join the receiving line."

No need to reply, only to act. I walk to my right, and, yes, there it is: a line of fine looking older people standing shoulder to shoulder, holding drinks, chatting, waiting.

A wedding? Is this a wedding?

"Negative," Dylan intones. He knows.

I approach what look like the end of the line, beside a nice-looking white man wearing a naval uniform and his petite Asian wife, who seems accustomed to accompanying her husband to ceremonies. She looks not too bored and not too excited. Both of them – as well as many others – are peering into a (disposable) mini-monitor. She doesn't notice me as I come nearer.

I look across the hall, past the dancers, to a raised platform, decorated with bunting and drapery. There's a long table running across the length, with maybe 20 people sitting at it, side-by-side, looking out over the others below them. The "head table," I believe it's called.

"Affirmative," I hear.

At that head table, near the center, near a lectern in the middle, I can see several men not dressed like the others. Instead of wool suits and neckties, these men are wearing pajamas. And headdresses. And moustaches and beards.

Arabs. The good kind. The ones allied with us against Brazil and Russia.

Am I imagining? Vice-President Mataphwa up there, too?

"No, you're not imagining. But you already knew that," Dylan says, amused and affectionate.

My eyes are fully adjusted to the theatrical lighting inside the Hall. I can see up there in the VIP section other important members of our government. Cabinet members – there's Lynn Stakely – and for sure a Senator or two. I recognize one of them very clearly. My step-father.

A cluster of guests, drinks in hand, wander away from the dance floor. In the space they leave behind, I can see the words "'nual Charity Ball," projecting from the table's side display screen.

"A fundraiser," Dylan says, *in a tone that
sounds like he's reminding me.*

*I know how this works. The Y$1,000-a-plate
redistribution plan.*

"That's a nice way to put it," Dylan
compliments me.

*The cause doesn't matter. Someone is trying
to do something good for someone else. That's what
matters.*

"Precisely," Dylan says. *He knows.*

*The Arabs rise from their seats across the
hall. I see them avoid touching women. I see them
shake hands with men. They pause to pose for pics
when asked, and then amble down and off the
podium, down to the level of the other guests.*

*I see them making their way with a small
entourage, a retinue of security personnel and
assistants, making their way across the room past
the dance floor and the tables and the chairs and
the spectacular (organic) flower arrangements,
making their way to the head of the receiving line,
where one of them, it seems, is the person everyone
is standing around waiting to receive.*

*Image-grabbers and documentarians stand
at a respectable distance behind the Guest of
Honor, capturing moments discreetly, particularly
the facial expression of the folks waiting in line
when they come face2face with the Main Man.*

*He bows to the women and shakes with the
men.*

I understand fully now who he is and what's about to happen, and it's all perfectly OK.

Several other couples have joined the line. I'm no longer last.

"Have you met the King before?" a pretty older white woman, someone like my mother's age, asks me, smiling. "The King of Arabia?"

Dylan in my ear, firmly: "Tell the truth."

"No," I answer, without hesitating. "But I'm really looking forward to it."

"He's a great humanitarian," she says, nodding. "A great supporter in the race for a cure."

"We're close," I say, sensing somehow that it's the right thing to say.

"Yes," the lady agrees. "So close to beating this thing. Do you suffer?"

"No," I say, telling the truth. "Not anymore."

"Oh, that's wonderful," she says, with a look I can't decipher.

The King of Arabia is ten people away now. I can see his face. His deep-set dark eyes, almost black. His black facial hair. Too black, too dyed. Most of his neck is covered by sheets of sheer fabric, but what's visible is fat and wide. He seems not very tall, around my height in heels. He has a nice smile, showing his teeth when he greets a well-wisher.

He's eight away. I reach beneath my dress, just like I've been trained. It's all perfect. Yes, there

*it is, flush against the hem, locked in place by the
condom ring. It's flawless. Everything is flawless.
The universe is perfect.*

He's six away. I've never felt better.

*He's four away. Slowly, deliberately,
carefully...I wrap my fingers around the magic
switch, like I'm grabbing my toe in an asana. The
switch feels like it always feels every time I touch it,
just like I knew it would.*

*He stops to chat. I watch. I don't judge this
man. I don't ask why he's been targeted. I don't
know this man. I don't hate this man. They haven't
made me – I don't have animosity toward this stout
old man, this alleged example of the best our
species can do, a member of the elite,* royalty. *I
don't hate this man. I have for him only love.*

*He's totally loved, but he's got to go. I don't
know why, but he's got to go. In the spirit of love.*

I love everybody. I do. I love everybody.

*He's two away, grinning at the Naval officer
and his wife.*

I love everybody. I love everybody.

*I'm so filled with love I want to cry. I love
the universe and everything in it – and my love, this
shining aching eternal love, reminds me that
everything – absolutely everything – is going to be
all right. Oh, yes. Oh, yes!*

I love and I am *love.*

I am love. I am love.

He stands before me. I can see my reflection in his eyes. I love him.

"Termite time! Land of the free," I hear Dylan announce in my ear.

I hear myself singing, "And home of the brave!" as I move the switch up-and-to-the-right.

Immediate silence…

Infinite whiteness…

Blindness, deafness…

And then a ripping of the air, a roaring boom.

And then I can see.

"Congratulations, Termite Joan," Colonel Flurk says, handing me a flute of Champagne.

I'm standing in the simulation studio. I'm in my heels. I'm wearing my dress. The Charity Ball has vanished.

I hear another boom – this one's more like a loud "pop," actually. All around the set, I see staffers pouring and drinking celebratory wine, toasting each other. "We did it," I hear someone say.

Flurk is standing where the King of Arabia was standing ten seconds ago, close enough for me to see the shine on his teeth.

"Here's to a successful simulation." He clinks his glass on mine. "You're going to be great tomorrow."

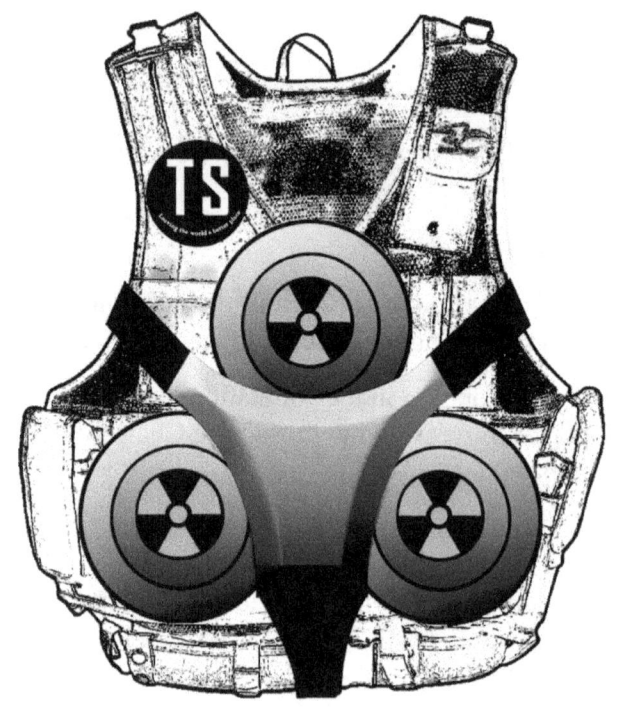

State of Mind

HISTORY MARKER: *it's 22:44 on December 30, 2090.*[56] *I'm still texthoughting® in my room, straight to draft. Arm working perfectly, but all feeds intentionally disabled. No interference, no contact with outside world.*

Not afraid. Not worried.

No concern.

It's all clear. Useful simulation. I know for certain what's going to happen in the morning, when they come to get me. I know what's going to happen after I'm all dressed up. I know how good I'm going to feel. I know what's going to happen at the *'naul Charity Ball* as the band plays and the girl sings and the New Year's countdown begins, and how it's all going to work out perfectly, for the best.

---

[56] Time-stamp verified.

This is where my likers and friends wanted me to be all along. The voters spoke clearly. The universe listened.

I know where I'm going tomorrow. And I know who's going to be there.

I mean, beside the King of Arabia.

I know, because these people, these honored guests and noble organizers and official sponsors -- they want me there! At least they pretended they did when they invited me.

"Please come! It will be great for everyone to see you again. I don't know why it's been so difficult to get everyone together." They've made me feel most welcomed, like I wouldn't even have to slip into their exclusive event through a secret back entrance. Like I could come in through the front door, and find my name card and sit down at a table with other cherished donors, and be treated like a member of the club, and chitter-chatter about everything except our shared sickness.

This is my birth tribe. We throw extravaganzas in grand public spaces off-limits to the public, charity balls that benefit untreatable diseases so we can avoid examining our own unique malady.

These are my brothers and sisters.

They're your brothers and sisters, too. They're part of our infinite global family. So thank you for caring about them the way you do any member of your family.

Be happy that there's still no cure for Lupus.

Be happy that people like my Uncles Jason and George and my step-brother Daniel, and my step-father the Senator and my mother Elaine are all intent on putting on a big show of how much they care about helping the ones who can't help themselves.

Be happy that they'll all be there.

By the time you read this, they're glamorous spectacle will be the biggest news of the Millennium.

Want to Know What I Think?

HISTORY MARKER: *it's 23:02 on December 30, 2090.*[57]

Do you want to know what I think? If you don't, just skip this. Scroll down.

I imagine all the investigators will want to know. They'll find clues to my "mindset" and evidence of whatever it is they want to prove. Never mind that I've spent, like, literally hours and hours over the past two weeks, thinking and typing this all in specifically so there would be NO QUESTION about my history and my motives. But, hey, we understand that Homeland Security is our country's biggest business, so folks gotta do what they gotta do.

I'll say it one last time: they can call me whatever foul names they want when I'm gone. But they can't *change the truth*, can they?

So, here. More raw data to mine. May you find what you seek.

---

[57] Time-stamped verified.

DOES JOAN GALT THINK HER PLAN WILL WORK?

I believe it will. I also know there are several ways that it could fail. It's entirely in God's hands now.

DOES JOAN GALT BELIEVE IN GOD?

Yes. I believe God is not an individual or a deity with special powers. God is the collective energy, harmonic vibrations, and mystery spirit of the entire universe. God is life.

DOES JOAN GALT SUBSCRIBE TO ANY RELIGION?

No. I was briefly exposed to Presbyterian propaganda by my well-meaning Dads, but mostly because the elite private school they chose for me included daily chapel. It never stuck. Yes, I do have a "mass disturbance" arrest on my record, but so do thousands of other girls caught up in our nation's zeal to stimulate the prison economy.

DOES JOAN GALT BELIEVE IN TRUE LOVE?

Yes. Oh, yes, I do. Forever and eternally.

DOES JOAN GALT HAVE HATE IN HER HEART?

No! Some self-loathing? For sure. Maybe more than most people, maybe less. Clarification: Although I despise the genetic code that defines who I'll become, *I don't hate myself*. And *I don't hate anyone else*. I strongly dislike some people, but I still love them. Everyone is my brother and my sister. Everyone is related to me, and me to them: we're all children of the same exploding star. We're all stardust.

DOES JOAN GALT THINK SHE'S REALLY ACCOMPLISHING ANYTHING?

This vexes me. I *know* I'm accomplishing something in the short-term. I'm definitely leaving the world a slightly better place than I found it. But long-term? If history teaches us anything, it's that while everything everywhere is constantly changing nothing ever really changes. Me? I'm nothing. I'm a footnote soon to be forgotten. But if there were thousands of girls like me, millions of us, all committed to improving the human race by refusing to reproduce babies that carry 47333-AR...

WHAT DOES JOAN GALT REGRET?

Nothing. I don't have time for regrets. The past can't be mended and the future can't be controlled. It's all just *now*, the golden present.

DOES JOAN GALT BELIEVE IN REINCARNATION?

Not really. But anything's possible, right? I mean, if an adopted girl, a bastard girl, can figure out how to fix our broken world, anything might happen. Scientists tell us that we're all receptacles for energy, for vibrations and pulses, energy arranged just so, into kittens and fireflies and calla lilies, into plankton and porpoises and paramecium. How the universe will rearrange "our" energy when we return ourselves to space and time is a mystery. But I don't think I'm coming back. At least I hope not.

DOES JOAN GALT BELIEVE IN PROGRESS

Yes. And evolution. And incremental changes for the better. But I like the standard definition of progress: "The movement toward social justice and universal harmony." So my Termite Squad service is definitely a sign of progress.

WHAT DOES JOAN GALT THINK *YOU* CAN DO TO MAKE THE WORLD A BETTER PLACE?

Get tested. When you know who you are, try to do the right thing.

One Last Document

HISTORY MARKER: *it's 23:46 on December 30, 2090.*[58] *I have time to share one last document. Seriously. Tomorrow is the day, and I really don't want to spend my final night on Earth texthoughting® this document. I want to vaporize and tantrasize, first with myself, and then with a memory-card filled with beautiful lovers who made me so happy I was born a woman. And then I want to sleep, just a few hours, enough to awake refreshed and ready. I want to be up in time to watch the sunrise one last time.*

And then I'll need to start paying close attention to everything and make sure I do what I have to do before they take my Armscreen™ and all my algo-chips.

So here goes...

---

[58] Time-stamp verified.

The Termite Squad:
My Official and Authentic Report

*Some will claim "the system" should have
noticed there was a problem with me, that I needed
to be flagged for full-time drone coverage. I
submitted this as my final paper for a Creative
Writing seminar I took 10 years ago, when I was
still a teenager, before I went off to The Harvard™
and* before I met my mother. *Premonition? String-
theory time jumping? Can't say. What I know for
sure is that I sensed a long time ago how my
relationship with my so-called "family" would turn
out.*

Joan, this is very nicely written
indeed but it is such a sad
ending! Very good work.

Mrs. Blesch

A-

The Unwanted Tree

By Joanie Galt

September 24, 2080

The Taylors, the family at the top of the hill, the ones with the best soil for miles around and the most sunshine warming their fields, they had a problem. Too many plants were growing in their excellent dirt!

Their business was corn. Corn was what they grew, and only corn. It was the crop that made the Taylor family rich. They were the richest family anyone knew. Corn was the reason. It was the *right* kind of crop for a family like them.

When birds dropped sunflower seeds and grape seeds and broccoli seeds, or when the wind blew in stray seeds from neighboring farms, the Taylors ripped out the unwanted sprouts and threw them away before they could develop fully. Better to save the space for more corn. The Taylors didn't want to grow unnecessary food in their corn fields.

One day when the Taylors were tending to their fortune, picking through their early Autumn planting beds, Mother Taylor shrieked, "Family, come look! We have a new baby!"

Father Taylor, and their son Junior, and Junior's Uncles and Aunties (Father and Mother Taylor's brothers and sisters) -- everyone gathered around Mother Taylor, who was bent over at the waist poking at the ground with a stick.

"Mother Taylor, what is it?" Father Taylor demanded.

She sighed and shook her head dejectedly. "I'm sorry to say that this new baby appears to be a tree."

"A tree? A good tree?" Junior asked.

"No, son," Mother Taylor said. "We don't want this tree in our perfect fields. It would take up space and rob our legitimate babies of their sun and water. This is a bad tree."

"How did it get here?" Junior asked.

"By mistake," Mother Taylor answered.

"I don't want this in my perfect field! Let's uproot the damn thing," Father Taylor suggested. He went to tug the baby tree out of the ground. It was only a foot high. He could do it with one hand. He gripped around the baby tree's slender main stem, the one that might grow into an impressive trunk with proper care and nurturing. But when he pulled up to rip the roots out of his exclusive soil, the baby tree wouldn't go.

"Stubborn little thing," he announced, pulling harder. "Ach! Damn! My back!" Father Taylor rubbed himself on the hip. "I hate this tree. I'll have to get a shovel for this thing."

The Uncles and Aunties had a suggestion. "Leave it be. We can just pretend it doesn't exist!"

Junior chuckled. "That's so silly, my family," he said. "This tree will eventually grow to be bigger than all the cornstalks in our field. Everyone will be able to see this from miles around, towering over our estate."

Mother Taylor looked at the baby tree in her family's dirt. "We can kill this unexpected life, or we can try to ignore it, or..." she shrugged, "we could love it like all the little babies we planted on purpose."

303

The family all laughed. "That is a funny idea!"

"We must return to our corn," Father Taylor said, getting serious. "Obviously, this tree cannot stay in our field. One day it will grow big and strong, and we won't be able to stop it from reaching toward the sky. One day, son, you might have the urge to climb in the branches of this tree, and you might fall. The boy is right: you can't simply ignore a bothersome intruder like this, because eventually a shovel won't do the job."

"We could see if it gives fruit of some kind," Mother Taylor proposed.

"Oh, Mother, you are a dear woman," Father Taylor said, tittering. "You know this tree wouldn't help our business. It would be a drain on our resources."

"But we have so much," Mother said, sweeping her hand over the endless fields.

He looked over their family holdings, the largest in the county, the finest land for miles around. He shook his head. "No. We can't keep it."

Just then, the little tree, bent and bedraggled, spoke to the family. "I did not ask to be brought to this field. God put me here. I know I will never give you corn. I admit I cannot make you richer than you already are. But if you care for me and help me grow, I'll invite birds to sit in my branches and keep watch over your fields. I'll give you shade to stand in when the sun is hot, and when it storms I'll shelter you from rain. I will dedicate my life to making your family happy and proud that they found me. You will feel that you received an unexpected gift from the universe."

The Taylors stood uncomfortably, kicking at the dirt, not looking at each other or the tree. Finally, Father Taylor said, "I'll get the shovel."

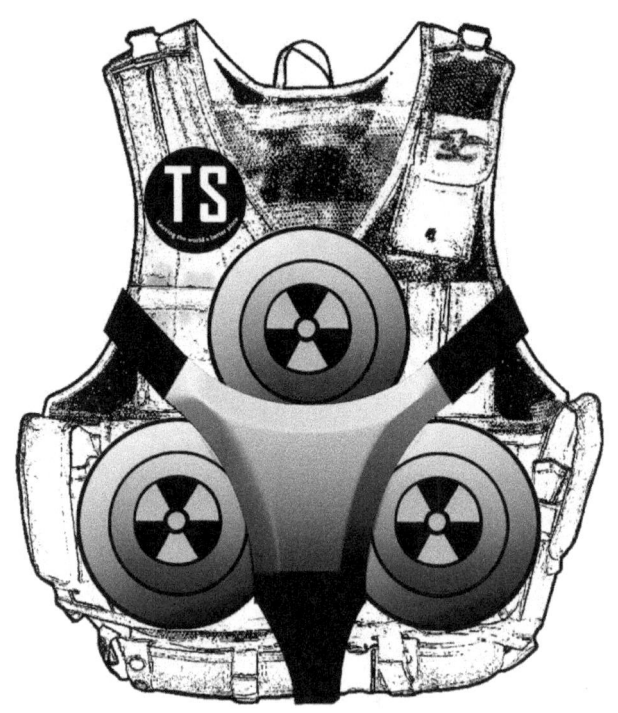

Almost Live, So You Can Be With Me for the Glorious Moment

HISTORY MARKER: *it's 08:58 on December 31, 2090.*[59] Last wishes coming right after this, writeeen thismrning, planned to have this worked out before they cmae so you could be withme when its happening but I swer I can hear a copter on my roof theyr coming, loveu all lobe you…trmte jn

[SCHEDULING LIVE PUBLISHING NOW]

Confirmation #6ULC372: AUTO-MESSAGE SCHEDULED SUCCESSFULLY. POSTING ON **01:01:00; 01-01-2091**

---

[59] Time-stamp verified.

Humble Request

HISTORY MARKER: *it's 06:44 on December 31, 2090.*[60]

If you're still reading this: THANK YOU.

You don't owe me anything. Nothing.

I'm doing this to be of service to our species, to our planet, and to the universe. I expect nothing in return. Nothing.

I'm not telling you what to do. You'll find your own path. I'm merely being the change, living the example, manifesting the goodness and love that vibrates through and around all of us.

I'm sacrificing myself for the greater good. Like a termite. In a perfectly aligned society, that wouldn't be a big deal.

Really, when you think about it…I mean, individually, we're all varying degrees of utterly

---

[60] Time-stamp verified.

irrelevant in the grand scheme. But if a few of us can inspire many of us…

What I'm saying is: I'm hoping something good will come of my early exit. So it won't have been a big waste.

I'm optimistic, but I'm also realistic. Jesus Christ died for all our sins yet we find increasingly perverse ways to thank him and his Father. *He just wanted us to love each other.* That's the challenging part for us, right?

Especially if we're infected from the start.

Jesus knew. According to the Gospels, he intuited the rich-person-getting-into-heaven problem *thousands* of years before science could identify the 47333-AR gene. You could say "some things never change."

Or do they?

Will they?

That's up to you. If you're reading this, you're one of the people who can change the world.

You won't let my death be in vain.

If you think I've done a good thing for our world, if I've left the home nest a little better than I found it, a little more secure for everyone else, then I shall depart this planet with a humble request.

Honor my memory by loving each other.

Honor my "sacrifice" by taking care of each other.

Be brave when the ill and deranged try to discourage you. Be brave. That's what I keep telling myself in these final minutes. *Be brave*.

Love your alleged enemies.

Love the lowest and the frailest, even as evil impulses encourage you to exploit them.

Love those who are different than you.

Love yourself.

Free yourself. Refuse to be a slave. Refuse to be a slave-owner.

Act with compassion and kindness and empathy for all living creatures – even the ones that must be humanely dispatched for the greater good. Then and only then will everything be right with the world.

Then "liberty and justice for all" will be more than a theory.

I'm going to die with a smile on my face, because I know *I've done what I can*. And that's all any of us can do.

Thank you. *Namaste*. I'm eternally grateful that you read these words. My hope is they'll be useful to you. Thank you, my true brothers and sisters, for giving me this opportunity to serve you with my one and only life.

I am blessed.

And so are you.

A Note From the Author

I'm a pacifist. I'm opposed to violence. Joan Galt's viewpoint is not mine. But, according to my way of thinking, she sure got one thing right: the world doesn't need more billionaires.

That seemed obvious to me when I wrote *The Termite Squad*, which, after all, is a kind of satire of American values. In the wake of the November, 2016 election, it seems that life is satirizing the book. The Very Important People have stopped their usual practice of renting governmental power; for the next few years they own it. And they will now do to the world – and all its inhabitants – whatever best conforms to their image of themselves as kings and queens, gods and goddesses, heirs to Genghis Khan and Cleopatra.

Should we be surprised if one of the little people, someone who has been made to understand how useless he is in the face of oligarchy, pulls a Joan Galt? Martyrdom awaits.

Between the first and second editions of this book, I didn't figure out the answer to the Greed Problem. I *do* know that if you bought this book on Amazon.com, Jeff Bezos became infinitesimally (but measurably) richer. And that's marvelous, isn't it? Once again, one of the most valuable members of our society was rewarded (monetarily) for being so wonderfully valuable. You might be tempted to say everything's working perfectly, according to plan.

One day soon, you might also think strapping on an EndVest™ could be a good idea.

Michael Konik
April, 2017; Los Angeles

The Author Acknowledges . . .

Writing a book is easy compared to publishing a
book. It takes one person, more or less, to compose
the text. It takes a legion to bring the text to readers.
I'm grateful for the encouragement given by a
constellation of helpful colleagues and supporters.
At the center of that galaxy, we find EggyPress.ca,
publisher Lance B. Colak and designer Eric W.
Bangle, who imagined a new (and highly
entertaining) way of presenting my work to the
world; Marissa Merrill, who lent her visage and
energy to bring Joan Galt to life; and my literary
agent, Uwe Stender of TriadaUS, who passionately
embraced *The Termite Squad* and introduced it to
the publishing industry. Thank you, friends.
You've done something wonderful.

Other Books by Michael Konik

Making It
Becoming Bobby
Reefer Gladness
The Smart Money
Ella in Europe
In Search of Burningbush
Telling Lies and Getting Paid
Nice Shot, Mr. Nicklaus
The Man with the $100,000 Breasts

www.ingramcontent.com/pod-product-compliance
Lightning Source LLC
Chambersburg PA
CBHW061128200626
46817CB00016B/396